Dancers & the Dance

Dancers & the Dance

STORIES BY SUMMER BRENNER

COFFEE HOUSE PRESS : MINNEAPOLIS : 1990

Some of these stories first appeared in the following magazines: Dance Scope; Sweet Little Sixteen: Jugend in den USA (published in Germany).

Cover illustration: Pablo Picasso, *Four Dancers*. 1925. Pen and ink, 13 ⁷⁄₈ x 10 inches. Collection, The Museum of Modern Art, New York. Gift of Abby Aldrich Rockefeller. Photograph © 1990 The Museum of Modern Art, New York, New York.

Back cover photo by Ruth Morgan.

The author would like to gratefully acknowledge Barbara Gates, Kimberly Duncan, and Felix Brenner for their respective contributions to this collection.

In "The Flamenco Dancer" the lyrics of the songs were excerpted from *The Art of Flamenco* by D.E. Pohren.

The publisher thanks the following organizations whose support helped make this book possible: the National Endowment for the Arts; Cowles Media/Star Tribune; Dayton Hudson Foundation; Minnesota State Arts Board; Northwest Area Foundation, and United Arts.

Coffee House Press books are distributed to trade by Consortium Book Sales and Distribution, 287 East Sixth Street, Suite 365, Saint Paul, Minnesota 55101. For personal orders, catalogs, or other information, write to Coffee House Press, 27 North Fourth St., Suite 400, Minneapolis, MN 55401.

Library of Congress Cataloging in Publication Data
Brenner, Summer.
    Dancers & the dance : stories / by Summer Brenner.
        p.   cm.
    Summary: A collection of twelve stories exploring the complex world of dancers.
    ISBN 0-918273-75-7   : $9.95
    1. Dancers–Fiction. 2. Dancing–Fiction. [1. Dancers–Fiction. 2. Dancing–Fiction. 3. Short Stories.]   I. Title. II. Title: Dancers and the dance.
PS3552.R386D3   1990
[Fic]–dc20   90-30312   CIP

Contents

To my teachers

Ella Baff
Hazel Bercholz
Eloisa Vasquez

and to his memory
James Tyler

O chestnut tree, great rooted blossomer,
Are you the leaf, the blossom or the bole?
O body swayed to music, O brightening glance,
How can we know the dancer from the dance?

— WILLIAM BUTLER YEATS

The Ballet Dancer

I THINK *ballet* was the first word that Francine ever said. Yes, it was. At least, that's the way I remember it. And that's the story that circulates once or twice a year among the members of our family. She was almost two years old at the time, and she pursed her lips together and said "ballet," only it was one syllable.

"Ballet," she repeated to please us.

I'm Adele, her favorite aunt, and she, I might add, is my favorite niece. I couldn't have been more delighted with her first choice of expression. If only I had had the presence of mind to have recorded it. Then I could have listened to that tiny voice today repeating, "Ballet, ballet, ballet."

Francine is eight now. Evidently she loves every kind of dance. She wiggles in front of television commercials and imitates the teenage boys in the subways who dance like robots and martians. I can't tell what it's supposed to be, but Francine loves it. She loves Fred Astaire and Ginger Rogers. But like me, Francine loves ballet the best.

Her mother, my sister, is sick of hearing about it. Bev claims that ballet is a shackled dance, tied to a worn-out tradition, an antiquated politic, a tyranny. Francine and I both leave the room when Bev begins these tiresome monologues. Francine is bored by them, and I'm dismayed. How could she–born from the same mother and, we may presume, the same father–want to degrade beauty and its greatest heritage at every chance? I can't fathom it. And I've silently vowed to protect Francine from it.

Even though Bev is disgusted by my encouragement, she hasn't interfered. She's afraid Francine will hate her the way we hated our mother for not encouraging us as children to do what we really wanted. For her it was science. For me it was music, clarinet to be exact. Anyway, Bev became a lawyer, and I work for Bloomingdale's as a window dresser. Our mother is alive and lives on Long Island. She thinks Francine should be a ballerina, no matter what it takes. It's her pleasure to buy Francine leotards, tights, tiaras, tutus, whatever she wants. The clerks at the Capezio store know us by sight. And everyone falls in love with the sight of Francine, pirouetting in front of store windows, arabesquing on the crosstown bus, chasséing by the fountains in Central Park. As far as I'm concerned, Francine is already New York's youngest star. Like I said, for her mother, my sister, it's a different story.

Every time Bev takes Francine into a bookstore, she says it's painful to watch. Why she should get a pain because her daughter wants to be something? Bev claims it's unhealthy, even dangerous, that Francine has such fixed ideas about her future. She says it pulls her apart to watch Francine take down the large photography books and study the poses of the great dancers.

Francine told her mother that she thought they should change their family name from Robbins to something that sounds foreign. I thought Bev was going to have a cardiac at that. Francine is a stubborn girl and insisted that even if no one else in the family goes along with her, she is going to call herself Robinotsky. She showed her mother a list of the great ballerinas — Olga Spessivtseva, Bronislava Nijinska, and in the case of Alicia Markova, she was born Alicia Marks. Bev says Francine studies the pictures of these dancers, turning the pages slowly and eating each magical feat.

"She sees a handful of prima ballerinas over decades and believes she's looking at herself in fifteen years."

"So?" I say.

"Well, what if that doesn't happen? What if she has to be a snowflake for the rest of her life?"

I know Francine has been planning big things for herself. At six she decided that she had to do well in school so she'd be permitted to travel for performances. She's never brought home a poor mark. I'm pleased to say her favorite books are the ones I've given her. Versions of *Pétrouchka*, *Coppélia*, *Swan Lake* are practically worn out from the number of times their pages have been turned.

Now that Francine is older, instead of picture books, I bring her biographies of important dancers.

She asks me how was it that when no one believed Anna Pavlova would ever get well as a child, she grew up to be a great ballerina. And Maria Tallchief, who was raised on an Indian reservation in Oklahoma, how did she find her way to stardom?

"Who made these things possible, Aunt Adele?" Francine's eyes fill with tears as she repeats the stories of their hardships.

I'm a little helpless with these questions. I don't know the answers. Sometimes I respond, "A great teacher." Or, "A mother, an aunt, someone like that." I think Francine wants to hear that each one of those stars prayed for it to happen and it just did. I think that's what she's doing now.

Francine is only a little girl, of course, but she's very serious. She doesn't enjoy playing with other children, especially her older sister, who's ten. Her sister, Celeste, takes after her mother. She's a tomboy. She runs around in pants all day, riding her bike up and down the sidewalk. Francine, I guess, takes after me. Everyone says she even looks like me.

When she doesn't have ballet class, Francine comes home after school, puts her scratchy records of Tchaikovsky on the phonograph, and dances by herself. Bev has told me that Francine also studies herself constantly in the mirror. This is the thing my sister tolerates least about Francine's fixation. Apparently Francine tries on her ballet outfits and poses for hours in first position, second position, third position, etc.

Personally, I see nothing wrong with it. "It's dressing up," I tell my sister. "That's what we used to do. It's what we're still doing."

"Maybe *you* are," she said in that accusing tone of voice. I told her to take a hike back to the courtroom.

Francine was born in April but her favorite time of year is December. Not for the presents, not for the snow, but, of course, for *The Nutcracker*. I've taken both her and her sister every year since Francine was three. The first time she was in a real theater, she stood in her seat and didn't blink, didn't budge. I thought it was the most remarkable thing I'd ever seen. I could barely watch the stage, I was so fascinated by Francine's concentration. Going home, she said she wanted to be one of the children who jumped out from underneath Mother Ginger's skirt.

So far, Francine has only gone to ballet classes in the neighborhood. I've discussed the situation with her teacher. Considering the child has such an unusual degree of enthusiasm, we've decided Francine should go to one of the more professional ballet schools in New York. I've even persuaded Bev that it's the right thing to do.

"After all, kids start early if they want to get anywhere, and why put Francine's talent at a disadvantage?" Those were my exact words to her mother, and she could hardly disagree.

Francine has known about the audition for several months, and she's been preparing, practicing combinations that are really beyond her ability. Even though I'm prejudiced, she actually does quite an impressive job. Her battement tendu is remarkable for someone her age.

I've completely enjoyed her excitement, and I've played a little at coaching myself. Just a few tips, especially with bowing. I showed her two different versions of a curtsy and an encore bow to the floor. And I taught her how to say "thank you" and "good-bye" in French.

"Au revoir," Francine says to everyone now—the grocer, the paper boy, the bus driver. My sister says I'm forcing affectations on her.

But that's ridiculous. "It's another language. You certainly can't object to her learning another language."

Today is the audition at the top ballet school in New York. Even four-year-olds have to audition to get in. Francine knows it's the best, I know it's the best, everyone in New York knows. Francine's stomach has been upset all week. She hasn't gone to school the last two days, and she's been complaining about headaches at bedtime. My sister said it's a case of nerves, and when she finally called the pediatrician, he said the same thing. The poor child must have lost weight during the week because when I went to see her last night, she looked frail to me. It was the first time that I had ever seen Francine sick. And they said—her mother and the doctor—that she wasn't even that. Anyway, poor darling, she brightened when she opened the package I brought her. A pink, striped leotard and matching tights.

"You'll be the best-dressed ballerina there," I whispered to her.

"Aunt Adele," that's what she has always called me, "merci, merci, merci."

I unwrapped her arms from around my neck and gave her a big good-night kiss. "You get some rest now. Tomorrow's your big day."

My sister really couldn't take the day off from work because of a court date, but I think it was her way of saying I should do the honors. I arrived at their apartment at three o'clock. We had one hour to go down and across town thirty blocks. No problem. I had already planned for us to take a cab.

Francine answered the door, wearing her linen party dress and black patent shoes. Her face smiled up at me, scrubbed and shining. Her teeth sparkled, and her doe brown eyes pleaded with me to make sure this was the most wonderful day of her life. I put my hand on the top of her head and smoothed several strands of hair back towards her ponytail. There she stood under me, and she was perfect.

"Now darling, you mustn't be disappointed if you don't get in the school."

"Don't say that. You don't have to say that. You sound just like Mother."

"I'm sorry," and I brushed my lips across her forehead. "Get your things."

Francine ran to the bedroom for her dance bag and her doll. In the bag were her new leotard and tights, a hair net for a bun, her ballet slippers, and a brush. She said her doll was for good luck.

"Break a leg."

Francine's eyes clouded and she backed away from me.

"That's what you say to someone going out on stage. It's good luck to say that. It really is."

Francine laughed. She understood that if you said something bad, then only something good could possibly happen.

Our cab drove across Central Park. It was a warm day, and children filled the park with their skateboards and kites and bicycles. Francine looked at them, and I could see how much apart she felt from their childish activities. She knew she had already resigned herself to giving up a childhood.

We stopped in front of a dingy brick building. The entryway looked as if no one swept, no one cared for it all. I could tell Francine had expected to see a hallway designed like an elegant stage set, but there was nothing to look at. Two brass cylinders of sand for cigarettes were placed between the elevators, and a disinterested doorman sat on a shabby armchair.

"Third floor," he mumbled.

The elevator door opened directly onto a large, brightly lit dance floor. Windows ran the whole length of one side of the studio, a baby grand piano stood in one corner, barres and mirrors were mounted on two sides of the room, and at the entry across from the skyline, several dozen small girls and their mothers sat on benches.

Francine looked as if her heart would burst. It was a beautiful room. The floors were smooth and warm, polished like glass, inviting her onto their surface to spin and glide and turn. She bent over to touch them with her hand as if it were a pond. The floors were spotless. And the mirrors faced each other so that one image multiplied a hundred times.

We were directed to a changing room on the left. Inside was a long green couch, benches, a large armoire filled with dance skirts, one shelf full of leg warmers, another filled with shawls. Old leotards were thrown in a pile on the floor and battered toe shoes hung from a row of hooks by the door.

In the dressing room, Francine had the same feelings of confusion that she felt in the lobby of the building. Things were so ugly and beautiful at once. She didn't understand. I wanted to tell her how much hard work it took to be a ballerina, how much sweat and physical pain. How the toe shoes were worn out because the feet in them had rubbed the satin away, sweated through the ties. And the leotards were faded and torn from the dozens of washings. I wanted to tell her that the costumes on stage were only adornments that happened after years of working very, very hard.

"It smells in here, doesn't it?" Francine held her nose.

"That's from all the perspiration. There's no window, and these dance clothes sit here until the dancers take them home."

Francine changed into her new leotard and tights. I twisted her hair up into a bun and sprayed down the stray wisps. We didn't say a word. Instead we watched the two teenage girls who were changing too. They pulled their hair back, threw their gum into the trash, put on their leotards with sweat shirts over them, pulled on their tights, their ripped leg warmers, and sweat pants. They complained about the heat. I wanted to suggest they take off some of their clothes, but I didn't think they'd appreciate it.

Francine and I walked through the hall, back into the sunny dancing room. The rows of large buildings behind the windows looked in on us like brick teeth, smiling through arched glass frames. At the piano the accompanist had started to play "Waltz of the Flowers." Francine's body swayed against me. I could feel her moving with the tune. She hummed and shuffled her feet in small ronds de jambes.

When the music stopped, Francine's hand grabbed tightly onto mine. Her palm was wet. If only she could do a solo for them all. I knew that's what she was thinking. If only the woman at the piano could have played the waltz again, then Francine would have lept out and done a dance to amaze us.

Instead, she wiped her hands on my skirt, and we waited for the audition to begin. She stared across the room into the mirrors that held reflections of herself and the other children. No one spoke, but the noise was constant of girls fidgeting and their mothers poking at their hair or straightening their bows.

Francine's eyes questioned mine. What would they have to do? Turns and jumps? Float like swans across the room? Raise their arms like wings and make a crown above their heads?

Madame T., the director of the school, entered the room with posture so erect that she resembled a piece of kinetic marble. Her features were chiseled as well, but her eyes and mouth were smiling. Her dyed black hair appeared plastered to her head, wrapped painfully tight in a twist at the back and held securely in place with a large tortoise-shell barrette. Her black eyebrows were emphasized with pencil. Her lipstick was stage red, and two spots of rouge contrasted with her white skin. Over her leotard she wore a black lambswool sweater tied at the waist and a thin, loose silky dance skirt. The only parts of her body that showed below her elegant neck were her bejeweled hands and her ankles that peeked between her tights and ballet shoes.

"I'm delighted to see you all here today." Her Russian accent was still evident. "I know you have come here because you want to dance the ballet." She emphasized the first syllable of ballet. "I want to give you your first lesson."

Madame T. placed her feet in first position, toes turned out and ankles touching. "Perhaps you already know what this is called. Perhaps you already know the five positions of the ballet. Perhaps you have already studied for one, maybe two years already." Francine looked at me and beamed.

Madame scrutinized the row of young faces.

"Before you can dance the ballet, you must do more than study. You must do more than practice. It is a dance which is not right for everyone. A dance which not everyone can do. Do you understand me?" Madame T.'s voice became very stern. The girls all shook their heads in affirmation that they did understand her. "It is a dance which only some of you are made to do." Here, the quality that had been stern became grave. "In this school, my school, we take only children who are made to dance very good ballet."

At this moment Madame T. waved towards the pianist, and she began to play a prelude. Francine had a record of Chopin as well, and again I could feel her heaving towards me in time with the music. Madame T. went to the barre to demonstrate a simple group of exercises. She went through each motion as if her entire body were connected to one center spot. The music stopped, but Madame T.'s body continued to pulse even in its stillness.

Then she waved her hand again, this time towards the children as if she were holding a wand. "I want to ask you to all come out here in a group. Yes, all of you. But first take off your ballet slippers. You may think this is very strange," she looked up at the adults on the bench, "but I am going to feel your children's feet. You must have a very special kind of foot to become a ballet dancer at my school."

Madame T. arranged the children in a line according to height. With each one she straightened their shoulders, aligned their necks with the floor, leveled their heads, and then stood before them. "You are all very, very good." Squirming started up and down the row. "But you must remain still. A good ballet dancer must be very still and listen very carefully." The children resumed their poses.

Madame T. began her inspection by stooping over the smallest child and picking up her left foot. She rubbed her arch, her instep, her toes. The child giggled madly until Madame T. was done. Then she was asked to sit down. The next child laughed herself onto the floor when Madame T. touched her arch. She too was asked to sit down. Francine was second to the tallest girl and had to stand twenty minutes for Madame T. to reach her. She didn't laugh, she didn't squirm.

"You are a very serious girl," Madame T. commented.

"Oui, Madame."

Madame T. felt Francine's left foot first, then her right, then went back to her left, back to her right. She repeated this inspection four times until Francine was sent back to the bench beside me.

"If I feel that your feet are not special for the ballet, you must not think this is a bad thing. It does not mean you have wrong feet or weak feet. I am able to tell at a very young age, even at four years old, three years old, if a child can dance the ballet. For me I do not take the child unless she is able to dance potentially well. For me I say, why should I teach a child that will only be an ordinary kind of ballet dancer? So the first thing I look at is the feet. That way I can be fair to you."

The room was silent. No one fidgeted, no one breathed. Everyone, girls, mothers, at least one aunt, waited the judgment to come. Some would be chosen, some would not. It was as simple and as terrible as that.

Madame T. walked down the row of seated children, looking into each of their faces. At least a dozen were waved towards the right side of the room. The rest of us were waved to the left.

"I'm sorry. I cannot take everyone. I have my reasons, and they are strong. The only thing I can say to you all is to keep dancing."

Most of the children were too young to recognize this sign of rejection. And most of the adults were too dumbfounded to protest. In fact, we all stood like cattle, waiting to be waved towards the elevator and out the front door. Everyone except Francine.

"What about me?"

"Yes, you," Madame T. smiled into Francine's tear-streaked face. "I wondered about you. You are stubborn and willing to do the work. That is good." Then she turned sympathetically to me as if she were a doctor, "But the feet are poorly arched, poorly formed, and in general, inappropriate for the study of the ballet."

"Look again!" Francine shouted. "Madame T., look at them again."

The other children and adults backed away. Madame T. picked up one of Francine's bare feet like a paw.

"I can only say that in eight years you would have many difficulties. You would be susceptible to injuries and incapable of great dancing. I'm sorry, my dear."

Francine walked in slow paces to the dressing room. She silently removed her leotard and tights and folded them like pieces of white tulle. She slipped on her undershirt, her linen dress, her black patent shoes.

"I'm ready." Francine spoke the way a stone might speak.

"I'm so sorry."

Francine stared at me, then through me, then pulled herself away out of the dressing room into the elevator, out of the lobby into the street. I followed, unable to lead, to command, to direct. I followed her to the corner, where she stepped into the back of a cab.

"We'll go to Schrafft's for a soda. Is that a good idea?"

Francine gave the driver her home address.

"We'll go to F.A.O. Schwarz and buy you a doll."

"No, I just want to go home. I want to see Celeste and my mother and my cat and my goldfish."

Francine folded and unfolded her hands, clasping her fingers. I placed my own hand over her two small ones. As soon as she felt me touch her, she crumpled. Two tears rolled over the rim of her eyes, and she stretched her neck around to watch the sign of Madame T.'s school fly backwards down the street.

The Closet Dancer

A VOICE ADVISED Eleanor Parkman to move to the mountains. When she went to bed at night, there were little whisperings, and when she woke up, they were there again. The voice told her to get as close to heaven as she could because she would soon be traveling there. Eleanor Parkman didn't put much faith in stories of hell and damnation, but after her husband Harold D. Parkman died, her hopes were raised that he was already sunbathing in the light of cosmic glory.

Harold and Eleanor had been married for forty-one years when he passed away. Harold had devoted all but two of those years to the postal service, rising from carrier to clerk to postmaster of Matting, Georgia. And Eleanor herself stayed busy as a third-grade schoolteacher Monday through Friday and a Bible teacher on Sunday.

As a young woman, Mrs. Parkman had a reputation as a strict disciplinarian. She was known to handle children that wouldn't listen. First, sit them in the corner, then stand them in the hall, and finally as a last resort, take a switch to their hands. However, as Eleanor grew older and the times grew harder, what with so much confusion in the world, communists taking over and anarchy marching in all around, Eleanor Parkman softened. She figured that her third-grade children were bound for hard times enough, and so she grew protective of them. Her face began to slacken, her temper sweetened, and she retired at fifty-eight with a great display of love from the entire community. Letters, photographs, and drawings poured in from all over the county from the various children Eleanor had taught. Even those who remembered her switchings could now admit that it had done them worlds of good.

Eleanor and Harold were never able to have children of their own, and even though they were sad, they had early on resigned themselves to God's will. They had each other, and in that they were devoted. Their evenings were spent at home, reading or playing cards with friends. Occasionally they went to Atlanta for a movie or out to the country to their favorite home-style restaurant. At Christmas they visited relatives in Florida. In August they fled the humidity and heat and went to the Blue Ridge Mountains. And during the spring and early summer, they puttered in their garden until dark. Eleanor cultivated the vegetables. Harold took care of the flowers.

Although Harold and Eleanor prided themselves on keeping up and had been the first of their friends to buy a television, a car with automatic transmission, a dishwasher, there came a time when they decided that modern times had gone too far. It was hard to pick up a front page and stomach what was being allowed to go on. Everything was in a state. The children couldn't get their attention on their school work. The minister at church was convinced that satanic forces were entering the doors and windows of every home. And at the post office Harold was besieged with complaints.

Complaints, mind you, not with the slowness of the clerks at Christmas time. No, it was the fuss being made over zip codes. And how the post office didn't know anymore where anyone lived unless it had a number attached to it. Crowds at the post office were complaining about the federal government butting in again, making it more difficult to get their packages off to loved ones, and having to look up number after number instead of getting on with their business.

Right after the New Year, Harold suddenly died, but it wasn't until spring that Eleanor got a little funny. It started in the garden. Eleanor went out to the flower beds and began talking to the blooms. The azaleas were just coming in, the jonquils just coming up. The dogwood blossoms formed a pink canopy along the fence. And the roses, Harold's favorites, were more aromatic than she ever remembered.

Eleanor sat on the ground in her house dress, her legs crossed under her, feeling the softness of the petals, examining the insides of the blossoms, and conversing with them as if they were the only friends she had left in the world. Actually, she was telling them all good-bye, for she had firmly decided that she would soon be moving away.

Eleanor's best friend, Louise, was the first to notice the strange behavior. Her concern came with good reason. Eleanor wasn't only talking to the flowers. She was talking to the furniture too. Louise overheard her. She saw Eleanor talking all over the house. Eleanor was, in fact, consulting with Harold, conversing with all the things they had shared and that still held parts of him. She was seeking his opinion, his comfort, and his advice.

Eleanor wasn't prepared for death's finality. She was bewildered. And a good antidote for that, she thought, was to bewilder herself completely. Go away, be a stranger, live simply, and seek heaven. It was the armchair in the guest room that had given her this last tidbit of advice.

"But you don't know anybody in Franklin," Louise protested.

"You'll come to visit often, won't you?"

Louise nodded enthusiastically. "But, it's such, such," and here her friend stumbled, "an uncommon thing to do."

Eleanor smiled. Yes, she thought, but there were other uncommon things about her. In the Parkman's two-story brick house, Eleanor's extensive collections were scattered among the rooms and halls. Boxes of pine cones, cases of butterflies, mixing bowls overflowing with wishbones – chicken, turkey, pheasant, goose. Stacks of handmade quilts, boxes of buttons, cases of trimmings and ribbons. And lately, that is, in the last eight years, Eleanor had taken to collecting figures, photographs, and paintings of dancers. She had dozens of them. Reproductions of

Degas's ballet figures, an etched couple delicately posed in the minuet, a plaster statue of Arthur Murray, ceramic Caribbean dancers with pineapples on their heads, carved hula dancers, a chipped sailor with legs askew in a hornpipe, and her favorite, porcelain Viennese waltzers.

When the time came to move, the dancers would go with her. There was much, however, that she would leave behind. Her friends advised her not to sell her house. Just rent it while she went to visit North Carolina.

Eleanor silently shook her head. She refused to discuss it. Eleanor's friends interpreted her stubbornness as a bout of depression. But, it wasn't that. Even though Eleanor had always appeared quiet, dependent, even shy, she knew herself quite differently. She was a closet dancer and had been one ever since childhood. At any moment of despair or confusion, since the age of seven, Eleanor would shut herself in a nearby closet and wriggle or sway until any unpleasant feelings were gone. In the early years of her marriage to Harold, she found herself alone dancing at least once a week, and since his death, she was in the closet daily.

Eleanor always kept her dancing a well-guarded secret, even from her beloved husband. It was the part of herself that she believed could never be shared, with Harold especially. He didn't dance and didn't care for dancing. This was his most disappointing quality since it was impossible for Eleanor to waltz or fox-trot with a husband who did not.

Now that Harold was gone, she would just do as

she pleased. She didn't think these thoughts with excitement or resentment. Things were simply bound to be different. And so was she.

By July Eleanor was ready to go. She had sold the house, given away the bulk of her belongings, and stored the items she would send for later. She had even arranged with the new owners to let her come in the fall for Harold's rose bushes.

To the dismay of everyone, Eleanor drove off one afternoon in her white Rambler station wagon. She traveled sixteen miles up the highway to the first motel by the side of the road, checked into a room, turned on the air conditioner as high as it would go, the TV as loud as she could stand, and cried for three hours.

It wasn't so much grieving as it was fear. All of a sudden the entire range of responsibilities that Eleanor had been carrying all her life slipped away. Replaced by possibilities. It was as if gravity had suddenly let her go and she was off the planet in darkness and the silence of space.

That night Eleanor slept a sleep she hadn't experienced since Harold died. And the next morning she jumped up vigorously and headed north through the foothills of the Appalachian range up into the winding country. It was gorgeous. Every foot of it, green and cool.

As Eleanor drove, she hummed. She listened to the country music station. She talked to Harold. She imagined how surprised he must be at her aptitude for daring. She grinned to think of him wondering what in the world had gotten inside her to make her do such a foolish thing as run away from everything she had ever known. She wondered about it too, but it was already like imagining another person. Someone she had known very well, intimately, but who was packed away. Teacher, wife, friend. If she did return to live in Matting, she could retrieve those people from between the layers of tissue where they were carefully folded and stored.

Eleanor stopped in downtown Clayton for lunch. There were only two blocks of Main Street, and on either side were the bank, the pharmacy, the hardware, the dry goods store, the florist, the shoe store, the mortuary, and a restaurant. Eleanor went to the soda fountain at the pharmacy for a grilled cheese and a cherry Coke. As she came out into the high, hot air, she heard someone call her name.

"Mrs. Parkman?" The voice wasn't actually asking a question, but the inflection of a Southerner naturally goes up in an inquiry at the end of a sentence. As if it weren't ever polite to make a declarative statement about anything.

Eleanor thought the sound was one of the whispering voices again, and ignored it. But then the question after the end of her name was repeated insistently, and she turned to see an unrecognizable figure standing at the corner by the only traffic light in town.

It was difficult to discern the face. There was a full crop of hair growing across the upper lip in an unruly mustache and from the chin down to the chest flowed a wild beard. The man's copper-colored hair hung down from his head in two braids, and the bill of an Atlanta Braves baseball hat was pulled low over his forehead. Everything about him was a reddish color. What she could see of his face was ruddy, his hair the color of a fox, and his eyes a serious roan. There she paused. The eyes resembled someone familiar.

Eleanor stared at the figure, and for a minute, or the kind of time that is called a moment because it has nothing to do with clocks or chronology, Eleanor's mind rolled across hundreds of third-grade faces staring up at her. Her eyes held onto the man before her, and his held onto her.

"You're Jimmy, aren't you? Jimmy Sears?"

"Yes, ma'am."

"Well, I almost didn't recognize you."

Jimmy grinned. "Yes, ma'am."

Eleanor's face beamed. Jimmy Sears had been a favorite. Then her face dropped off into concern. It was clear something unusual had happened to Jimmy.

"How you doing, anyway?"

Jimmy nodded politely and then tugged the baseball cap off his head. His thick hair looked brassy in the sun.

"I'm doing fine now." Jimmy's eyes lowered shyly.

It was his combination of shyness and enthusiasm that Eleanor remembered. Jimmy had rushed into the classroom the day after Easter with a baseball hat on his head, a baseball glove in one hand, a bat in the other, tripped over the desk, sprawled on the floor, cut his lip with his front tooth so bad that he had been sent to the hospital for seven stitches.

"Still wearing your baseball hat?" This was also a declarative statement.

"Yes, ma'am, only then it was the Atlanta Crack-ers."

Only then, it was a flat top. Eleanor looked with dismay at the hair Jimmy Sears had grown himself.

"I was sorry to hear about Mr. Parkman."

"You heard about him?"

"Yes, ma'am."

Jimmy's parents had moved away at least ten years ago.

"My mother's sister, Jessie Wallace, still lives in town, and she passed the news along to me."

Eleanor heard the concern in his voice. "Yes, it was too lonely in the house to stay."

"And so you moved?"

"Well, you might say I'm in the act of moving right now." Eleanor pointed to her crammed station wag-on. "I'm moving up to the mountains."

"That's where I live too. I come down here to Geor-gia to do my banking, but I prefer to call myself a citizen of North Carolina."

"So you're driving back today?"

"No, ma'am." And then he said shyly, "I don't drive."

"You take the bus?"

"No, ma'am. I don't like the smell."

"Well?" Now Eleanor remembered that Jimmy had been one of those smart but slow kinds of children. There were, of course, the slow and dumb ones. And the smart and quick. The most unsettling were the fast and dumb, bound for serious mischief. But the most baffling were the smart but slow children like Jimmy. They were bound for a religious calling.

"Sometimes I hitchhike, and sometimes I walk."

"All the way from North Carolina?"

"Well, we're almost at the state line. And I like the walk. I can take the Appalachian Trail almost the whole way. It only takes me a couple of days."

Eleanor looked at Jimmy with curiosity. He certainly had turned out uncommon.

"Well, you're welcome to a ride in a car if that's what you want to do."

"Yes, ma'am. I'd be grateful."

Eleanor looked straight above Jimmy's head at the sky. She hoped Harold was watching her authentic adventure. Watching her unfold in a new way in a new town, talking to someone who looked like a foreigner, whom she had just invited into the car with her.

Eleanor wanted to giggle out loud, but instead she composed herself into sixty-two years of Eleanor Bolin Parkman, forty-seven spent every Sunday at First Baptist, forty-one married to Harold D. Parkman, and thirty-eight in the classroom of Habersham Elementary.

Jimmy's home was a trailer on a bald spot of land at the top of a mountain. The spot looked to be a perfect circle surrounded by tall, straight pines. Mountain laurel and patches of blackberries competed for the strip of land next to the drive, and tomato plants tumbled in profusion next to the house. There was a rock garden built up from a small man-made pond, and chickens roamed the yard freely.

Down to the south was town and up to the north was a ski resort and the Cherokee Indian Reservation. To the west was the long, slow stretch of valley that signaled Georgia, and out to the east were the blue silhouettes of mountains that sloped into the plateaus of central North Carolina.

"Fourth grade was my worst year in school." Jimmy began. "That was right after I had you." Jimmy figured he'd start with everything that had happened since he last saw her. "Daddy lost his job at Lockheed, and Mother took to working over in Roswell. They gave us dog tags to wear that year and told us in case we were bombed by the Russians and didn't have a face anymore, they'd be able to tell our parents we were dead. By fifth grade Daddy had his job back and things were normal again."

Eleanor smiled sympathetically. For the first time since Harold's death, she felt relieved. Not for one instant that he was gone, but rather that she was having herself such an adventure.

Jimmy told Eleanor Parkman as much of his life's sorrows and joys as he could cram into the ninety minutes it took to drive from Main Street in Clayton to the trailer at the end of a long, dusty, and poorly maintained road.

"What do you do up here in the winter, Jimmy?"

"I got the dogs, ma'am."

Jimmy pointed to a six-foot chain-linked kennel under a shady cliff.

"If it gets too bad to walk, I just hitch 'em up to the sled."

Jimmy waved at the half-dozen Husky mutts, and they barked back in unison.

Eleanor had stayed amazed almost from the minute Jimmy had started to speak.

"I know I talked your ear off, Mrs. Parkman. Can I get you some iced tea?"

Since the year Eleanor had been Jimmy's teacher, his trust in her had remained fixed and unquestioning. In fact, this trust ignored everything that had happened to make him a grown man and her an old woman.

Eleanor and Jimmy sat on the stoop of the porch that went around all four sides of the trailer. They sat silently, both looking at the large trees, both aware of the sound their breathing laid across the stillness. Eleanor felt she ought to make a move, invent a destination, leave Jimmy to his chores, and get on with her business. But she couldn't budge.

"It's a pretty spot, Jimmy."

"Yes, ma'am. I found my home here." Jimmy started to laugh. "Mrs. Parkman, Mrs. Parkman, sitting on my front porch. I don't get many visitors and to think that one of them is you."

"It is quite a coincidence, isn't it?"

"Nancy Rae comes up here to see me sometimes. She's my cousin who makes ceramics to sell to the tourists from Florida. And I have a friend from the war who lives in Asheville. He and his family make it over the hill two or three times a year."

"You were in Vietnam, Jimmy?" Eleanor had seen a few former students who came back from the war different in the head. They all had a look in their eye that she had never seen before, not in Harold after the Philippines and Guam, not in her brother after Korea. The men who came home from those wars had forgotten everything but the good parts.

Eleanor peered into Jimmy's eyes. They didn't have the haunting in them that some of the young men had.

"No ma'am, they wanted me over there, but I told 'em I wouldn't be able to make it." Here, Jimmy laughed a good, deep laugh. "My friend over in Asheville was another one like me. He made 'em think he was so crazy they'd have to keep him tied up in a strait jacket through basic training."

"And what did you make 'em think, Jimmy?"

Jimmy could hear Mrs. Parkman's schoolteacher voice asking the question. He was embarrassed that he had made her so uncomfortable when they had been having such a good, relaxed time.

"Ah, let's not talk about it. It's over now, anyway."

Jimmy reached his hand inside the trailer and lifted out a photo album. He opened the book to a large picture of his face. It was as pale and flabby as white bread. Its shape and color resembled a biscuit, and his red hair cuddled his face in the shape of a bowl. Below the hairline, his lips were insolent and his eyes warm. The color of his eyes had a ruddiness that matched his hair and skin.

"Guess I looked kinda different then?"

"I reckon you did, son."

"That's when I went to art school in Atlanta. My mother believed I was gifted, but she wouldn't let me come home till I cut my hair. Daddy wrote me out of his will, said I was all kinds of unnatural things. He didn't have any money to disinherit me from anyway."

Jimmy paused as if he were back in the third grade,

struggling to add triple digits. "That's when I thought I knew it all." Jimmy smiled down at the image. "I went through hard times, Mrs. Parkman. Don't I look like I know it all there?"

"Yes, Jimmy, I can see that."

"Are you too tired to take a little walk? Just up to that ridge over there where the dogs are?"

Eleanor rose slowly to her feet, and Jimmy grabbed two walking sticks by the side of the porch. Eleanor peered into the back of her car as she passed by, filled with the souvenirs of her memory—a box of clothes, a box of her collectible dancers, a bag of books, and food. She made a wish for Harold in the sky. She wished that if he were watching, he understand what was happening. A little thing inside Eleanor skipped, and she could feel herself wanting to dance, not from despair or confusion, but from joy.

For a moment Eleanor considered that maybe she had already died and gone to heaven. She looked around. She and Jimmy had climbed a considerable way. They stood silently, staring at the sides of the hills. The view was breathtaking, the air newborn. Eleanor looked neither forward nor back in time. Her eyes scanned the groves of hardwood trees—the oak and ash—that made the hills look blue. She spied her car and Jimmy's trailer a hundred yards below. Birds soared above, and the sun dipped slightly to the west.

"Mrs. Parkman?" Jimmy's voice came from far away, as if it were out of a dream.

"Uhhhh?" Eleanor felt so peaceful it was a great effort to speak.

"I told 'em I was a closet dancer."

Jimmy's eyes screwed into Eleanor's face, hoping she wouldn't try to avoid him.

"Who, Jimmy?"

"That's what I told the draft board was wrong with me, ma'am. That's what I said to make them think I'd be a poor soldier."

Eleanor Parkman had resumed her gaze at the mountains. Her eyes wandered back and forth across the ridges at the top of the peaks.

"Jimmy, you said the right thing, didn't you, son?" Her left hand reached out and patted Jimmy's shoulder. "Exactly the right thing."

The Flamenco Dancer

"WHAT do you want?" Susan asked the question coldly, as if she were talking to a wall. She lowered her eyes into her drink, then let her body sink slowly back into the chair, waiting an answer.

Bernadette stared across the table at the woman's face, and the question floated between them like musical notes. "Susan," she thought. "This is Susan. He calls her Susan too. It's a pretty name, a soft name."

Bernadette repeated the question to herself, "What do I want?" And with each repetition, a different answer came to her.

"What do you want with him?" This is the question Susan wanted to ask, but she couldn't bring herself to acknowledge the man who had brought them together.

The question circled around Bernadette like lights from the candles on a birthday cake.

"Now make a wish, Bernadette." She stood over the candles ready to blow them out, trying to condense everything she wanted, everything she had ever wanted into one wish.

Finally, she took a deep breath, and looking Susan directly in the eye, she said, "I want to dance."

Susan's throat constricted, and she thought, "Oh, God, don't let me cry." She had anticipated something else. She had expected Bernadette to be brash. To declare she wanted to live with Edward, marry him, bear his children. She had expected Bernadette to say that she wanted to steal Edward away from her.

Susan looked down at the hand-painted tiles on the floor of the Café Firenze. She was trying to hate this Bernadette, but her answer had rung so true. Instead, it made her wish that she were away. Far away from her own life.

*

Yo como tú no encuentro ninguna,
mujer, con quien compararte;
sólo he visto, por fortuna,
a una en un estandarte
y a los pies lleva la luna.

I won't find another woman
to compare with you;
I have only seen one
on a pedestal
with the moon at her feet.

Bernadette Dominica Lee's dressing room mirror was encircled with a dozen bald light bulbs. Bouquets of silk flowers, photographs of Carmen Amaya, and cards of assorted admirers covered the frame. On the dressing table were stacks of eye shadow cartridges, cold creams, lipsticks.

Yards of costumes hung in the rear of the room, full skirts of turquoise and white polka dots for *alegrías*, black velvet for *soleares*, and red taffeta with a train for *bulerías*—the triumvirate of flamenco dance.

Bernadette's lids didn't blink as she applied the layers of mascara, a fuchsia color over the eyelid, splashes of rouge on the cheeks. Whoever it was staring back at her made no impression. She was neither beautiful nor ugly, rich nor poor, kind nor cruel. No, she was a masque who every evening slipped out of one skin into another.

Bernadette inspected her reflection for smudges and, after securing a sequined rose in her dark hair, stood up, her skirts and petticoats swishing as she walked into the hall to wait for the next show.

> *Cuando pases por mi vera*
> *When you pass by me*
> *forget that you have loved me*
> *and don't even glance my way.*

Outside the dressing room Bernadette held onto a doorknob, practicing the scales of her footwork. Toe, heel, toe, heel, toe, heel—her feet drilling so fast, it was impossible to see the distinction between the back and front of the shoe. She was up to fifty beats per minute, and at maximum speed her feet sounded like tiny automatic weapons.

Rudy stood away from the dressing areas, talking to guitar students who had stopped by for the midnight show. The other guitarist, Rocco, had slipped away to the bar for a tray of glasses and a bottle of red wine.

Twenty minutes till show time. A pack of cigarettes was passed among the performers, and derogatory remarks exchanged about one of the regulars, Jerry, who showed up every weekend. An ex-jockey, he was loud and alcoholic. Unfortunately he lived nearby. Jerry bragged that he was cousin to a Mafia earl and said if his calling hadn't been horses, maybe he would have been a great flamenco dancer. He flirted with the performers from his seat in the audience, left small tips in the bottom of his wine glass, threw silk scarves onto the stage.

Earlier tonight Rocco had become so aggravated with Jerry that he had shouted from the stage, "Keep your clapping to yourself."

Now an hour later Rocco was still complaining about the stupidity of a goat who thinks if he claps, then that's all there is to it.

"I'm right, aren't I, Bernadette? Why should we permit him to clap out of *compás*? You, I, all of us studied our *palmas* for years, didn't we?"

Bernadette's face was a grin. She liked Rocco. She liked his bad moods the best. Jerry was going to have him going all night, and now it was more a joke about Rocco than anything else.

Of course, she had studied for years. She had practiced *palmas* on the bus, in the car, when she walked to school, when she sat at home, anywhere she could. To keep up with the timing of the rhythms, the *com-*

pás, her *palmas* had to be perfect. No less. And like all of them, she had a pride and a respect for the complex percussion instrument of flamenco.

"And you're a great *palmista,* aren't you, Bernadette?"

Bernadette nodded affably. "Sí, Rocco, sí." She was thinking again about the phone call from Susan. That had taken some nerve.

*

"Is this Bernadette Lee?" The unfamiliar voice was too loud to be friendly.

Bernadette's face darkened. Occasionally a fan tracked down her home phone number and bothered her. But this was unprecedented. This was a woman.

"Who is this?"

"This is Susan Harvey, Edward's wife, and I would like to make an appointment to talk with you."

"I can talk now." Bernadette said coolly as her heart thumped in her head.

"Not over the phone."

"Why not?" Bernadette put her hand over the receiver and motioned Edward out of the room.

"I have something to ask you." Susan said, her voice still loud and agitated. "Can we meet at Café Firenze tomorrow at four?"

"Maybe."

"I'll be there," and then the phone clicked off.

Bernadette continued to warm up her feet and ankles with rudimentary footwork. She warmed up her hands too, rotating her wrists in complete circles, clapping in small, quiet beats, her palms raised to the front of her chest. Then precipitously Bernadette lifted her knee and the hem of her layered skirt flew like a geyser past her head. She grabbed a ruffle below her hip and made a turn. She turned again, arching her head and back towards the floor behind her. Then just as suddenly she halted, adjusted her stockings and the straps that secured her shoes, and pressed back the strands of hair that had fallen out in the turn.

Behind Bernadette stood Esme, their guest singer from Granada. Esme was a large woman, fifty-five and gusty. She was tall and broad with a pile of hair hennaed the color of Burgundy wine. Esme wore a plain black dress and an embroidered shawl as large as a tablecloth. It fell around her shoulders, and its fringe dropped to the floor. Above the shawl beamed Esme's smile and a front row of gold caps.

The ensemble gathered closer together. Rudy balanced his guitar on his knee, tuning each string. Rocco finished off the wine and ran to the bar to grab another bottle, laughing. "What's dance without wine?" What's flamenco without a drunken guitarist?

> I asked a wise man
> if love is good or bad;
> the wise man had never loved
> and knew not how to respond.

Bernadette stepped from the hall into the tiny foyer by the stage. The audience was packed onto the benches. Electric candles emitted a soft light from the corners of the boxlike room. Scenes of life in Seville were painted on the wall – shuttered windows behind wrought-iron balconies, veiled señoritas, cavaliers holding guitars and swords. Velvet sombreros, gigantic paper flowers, two dozen pairs of colored high-heeled shoes hung from the ceiling. Blue smoke curled from the audience towards the light, and waiters with trays of glasses entered and exited through the same door as the performers.

Rocco yelled, "Bernadette! Rudy! Esme! Carlos! y Marie!"

Each of them yelled back with whistles and exaggerated theatrical laughter. The stage sounded like an aviary.

"Rudy, eso! Bernadette y Carlos, porque no? Sí, Marie. Eso flamenco! Eh? Eh, eh?"

The confusion of sounds was the ticket the performers used to transport themselves instantly across the North American continent and Atlantic Ocean to Spain.

"Sí, Esme. Canta como un pájaro!"

Transport them to Andulusia where flamenco could spontaneously erupt in any bar, at any corner. Where flamenco meant a way of life, a way of narrating experience.

On stage they each took a seat. The banter continued. Then slowly, softly, the rhythms of the two guitars started. Up from the hollow of wood in the instrument came a sound, a creak that could have originated in the center of the earth. It was Esme's voice, singing as if a fish bone were stuck in her throat.

Dos corazones a un tiempo
Two hearts
are being weighed on a scale;
one asking justice,
the other—vengeance.

Were I to find out, companion
that the sun that shines offends you,
I would fight with it
although it cost me my life
aunque me diera la muerte.

Bernadette looked into the faces on the first row. Jerry was clapping softly to Esme's singing. Next to him was Edward Harvey. Bernadette lightly blew him a kiss with her eyes, and Jerry pointed to his chest to ask if it were meant for him.

Esme's voice merged with the guitar as she sang the words of the *alegrías*. Bernadette danced simply, playfully, on the stage. It was a gay song, despite the words. Bernadette kicked, she spun, she lifted her skirts, she danced faster, and as the music rose like a tornado, she suddenly stopped. On the beat the guitar stopped too. It was the first "break," and both she and the guitarist paused there. Then slowly she began again, until the next break. And so the *alegrías'* loud celebratory madness spiraled towards the ceiling, and the room felt as if it were shrinking in its frenzy.

*

Bernadette arrived at the café just after four. She recognized Susan immediately. She was sitting against the wall crouched like an animal in hiding. From the neck down she was covered with an expensive plastic raincoat and around her face her streaked blond hair hung in stylish disarray. Susan stirred the foam of her cappuccino with a finger, flicking her eyes from the street to the door.

Bernadette walked straight to the coffee bar for her usual—a double espresso with a twist of lemon rind. As she approached the table, her eyes locked for a second into Susan's face. In that instant it was as if she took in the whole world. In the distance was Edward and his decision to stay in a disappointing marriage. Behind him was Susan's own years of neglect by her husband and their absence of children. And facing them both was Bernadette, frozen, holding a demitasse. Bernadette saw that Susan's lips were narrow and ungenerous, but her eyes were gray and soft like her name. Her eyes were pleading that one of them should disappear from the earth, forever.

"I'm Susan," the woman said loudly.

"I know." By contrast Bernadette's voice was quiet. She hadn't expected to feel so overwhelmed with sympathy. "I recognize you."

"How?"

"The photo in Edward's wallet. He showed me once."

"Why?"

"I asked him."

Susan bit off a piece of skin from her lower lip. She didn't want to imagine that Edward mentioned her.

Or had shown her photograph to a stranger.

"Does he discuss me?" The words were barely audible. It was as if she had been carried into bed with them.

"Edward and I are friends." Bernadette tried to make her voice casual. "We speak on the phone. Sometimes I see him after the theater and we have a drink. No," she finally said, "he doesn't discuss you." She was surprised at how factual she sounded. Bernadette chased her espresso with a swallow of ice water. "He doesn't want to leave you either. He doesn't want that."

A large tear dropped from Susan's eye onto the milky foam of her coffee. "Why should you be telling me these things?"

*

On stage at all moments the sadness that prefigures everything flamenco is apparent, even in the gaiety of the *alegrías*. Bernadette drew the audience, the guitars and singer, the dancers, the waiters, the building, and the street itself into one continuous swirl of arms and legs, skirts and petticoats, before the motion of her body stopped one final time.

"Eso, Bernadette! Eso! Eso!"

Bernadette smiled down at Edward, and he touched his lips.

"Darling," she read from his mouth. "My darling."

Carlos rose for his *zapateado*. No music, no song, only footwork. Carlos began with the muffled beat of his palms and the slow tapping of the nails from the heels of his boots. As he accelerated, his gypsy feet bent rhythms out of the floor and created a sound that came from another time. Hundreds of centuries and thousands of horse hooves on dirt and cobblestone, in towns, at bull rings, across country highways.

Carlos lifted his chest and held his hand inside his vest over his heart. He walked, then ran towards the beloved, away from the pursuer until he was finally caught in a wild stampede. The equine stance of Carlos's body mirrored the shift of his gait across the stage. The horse in him was apparent. The gypsy in him was apparent too as he traveled with his tribe from India and Afghanistan, through Persia and Arabia across North Africa and Eastern Europe, west to Spain.

He and thousands of others had learned the trade of horses. They had harnessed them to pull their carts, used them as currency, and were reputed everywhere to be experts with horses—trainers, traders, thieves. And alongside the horses, the stories were born and raised.

Carlos's chest thrust out proudly with this knowledge, his waist drawn in and cinched with a wide sash, his head lifted high. These served to pridefully reveal the extremes of flamenco experience— love, loss, death.

Carlos didn't bow. Instead, he turned away from the audience as if they weren't there, as if he were at home. He walked casually back to the bench and resumed his place next to Esme.

*

"What do you want?" Susan finally extracted the words from her gut where they'd been boiling for several weeks. She had managed to make the question sound clinical.

Bernadette sucked on the bitter lemon rind.

"I want to dance." It was the truest thing she could say about her life.

Susan reached over to gather up her things. This meeting had been a very poor idea, she decided.

Bernadette made no motion to leave, no movement to let Susan pass by. "He isn't in love with me, you know. He isn't. He's in love with the way I dance."

*

Yo como tú no encuentro ninguna,
mujer, con quien compararte;
sólo he visto, por fortuna,
a una en un estandarte
y a los pies lleva la luna.

I won't find another woman
to compare with you;
I have only seen one
on a pedestal
with the moon at her feet.

After Rocco and Esme's duet, it was time for the last solo performance of the evening. Although barely evident, Bernadette was beginning her *soleares*. *Soleares,* the dance dancers love the most, the *cante* singers and guitarists claim as the deepest and sweetest theme. *Soleares,* the Sierra Madre of flamenco. Honey and limestone, the song is low in the throat, almost unutterable in its sadness. The dance is sad too, with no remorse, never self-indulgent, seldom resigned.

The song began softly, but the music didn't sound as if it could have come from two hands on one guitar. It sounded as if it were smuggled out of plaster and straw walls, bird nests, graveyards, moss. It sounded as if it were music that had to be played, as if the movements of the dancers were the parts of a story that had to be told.

Bernadette's dress was fitted and black, and her hair was slicked back in a knot. The only adornment was a crucifix strung high on her neck. She dressed as if she were in mourning.

Slowly Bernadette stood up. Count to fifty slowly, and she was still rising. Then she dashed in a few brisk steps to the center of the stage and executed a ferocious stomp. Her arms zigzagged in an esoteric sign, and the spotlight came up. Everyone held their breath, and Esme kept singing.

> *Lo gitano*
> *va en la masa de la sangre*
> *y en las rayas de las manos.*

> *That which is Gypsy*
> *is found in the surge of blood*
> *and in the grooves of hands.*

Voy como si fuera preso;
I go as a prisoner;
behind me my memories,
ahead, my thoughts.

Bernadette began marking the next phrase of the dance.

Detrás camina mi sombra,
delante, mi pensamiento.

Pacing the floor in curious and grand gestures of despair.

What did it mean to dance these stories over and over? Songs of a people wandering with their horses, guitars, and their beautiful, dishonest faces? Given to swindle as the only recourse to banishment. Given to fighting and singing, drinking and loving. Tragedy for what? Loss for what? Honor for what? For something for which there are no words? For poverty, for madre, for revenge? For the story and the song? For death itself and for testimony to the chronicles of existence? Flamenco was the single property of the most dispossessed of people.

Bernadette swept the sweat off her face with her skirt. Peasant empress, she danced, and no one breathed. Finally, the singing stopped, the last rain of footwork subsided to a slow extenuated walk down the four steps from the stage and out the swinging doors towards the hall and dressing room. There was an atomic silence, and then the inside of the wooden box began to roar.

"Bravo! Bravo! Bravo!"

"Eso, eso, eso!"

"Bernadette! Bernadette! Bernadette! Bernadette!"

She walked back humbly to the stage. It was time to finish with an ensemble display of *bulerías*. The wild *bulerías*. Swift, burlesque, flashy, obscene.

> *Tengo en mi casa un jardín*
> *in my house I have a garden*
> *in order to sell flowers for you*
> *if bad times come*
> *vender yo flores pá ti.*
>
> *If we were in a room together*
> *I would do anything for you,*
> *even take poison.*

Esme's voice was as shrill as a toy whistle.

> *Your mother says nothing;*
> *she is one of those who bites*
> *with her mouth closed.*
>
> *Con la boquita cerra.*
> *Con la boquita cerra.*

Rocco waved a bandana in front of Esme's breasts. Carlos swatted Bernadette's behind. And Rudy took up the end of the fiesta parade. The show was over.

Edward stood outside the dressing room, waiting. He had never seen Bernadette dance like she had tonight. She had held them all, the entire room – the entire universe for that matter – in the motions of her body.

"Bernadette," he wanted to say her name privately. He wanted to admire her alone. "You were extraordinary." He bent over and passed his hand across her forehead. "Eso."

Bernadette kissed him hard on the lips. "I saw you," she laughed. "You burned a hole through me."

Arm in arm they crossed Grant to Columbus into Tosca's. The late-night crowd had congregated at one end of the polished bar.

"I'll take a shot of scotch, straight up."

"Make it two."

"It was good tonight, huh?"

"There was never anyone who danced like you."

In America nobody danced flamenco to be a star. Bernadette would tell you. "It's my love, you know," she said. "Love for abusing my feet with hours of practice, banging and breaking the heels of my shoes." Suffering shin splints and bruised soles from the footwork, repeating endlessly the exercises to loosen the wrists, hold up the arms, raise the torso and neck.

"To you and your dance," Edward clinked his glass to Bernadette's and swallowed.

"I get so sick of it sometimes. It's possible. Just like you get sick of anything, even the best things." Bernadette had decided not to tell Edward about her meeting with Susan.

"Even the people you love?"

"Sometimes."

Sick of the meager glamour, the meager earnings, the charading of gypsy life. Sick of loving something that didn't exist anywhere anyway. Sick of imitating a descendant of a bunch of rags in an Andalusian hut.

Bernadette ordered a second drink. Behind the row of bottles she caught her reflection, thick features and poreless skin that looked closer to fifteen than thirty. Her face was unusual, but on stage it was her body that moved its observers. Its long trunk with an unnaturally small waist, large breasts, muscular legs, sinewy arms, and delicate hands—these served as a base for her immobile face.

Above the precise motions of her body was her still expression—a long, wide nose, a sensual lower lip accented by the scar from a fall, egg-shaped brown eyes that pleaded, rebuffed, then closed. Few ever got close enough to enjoy the sharp brain. It was now working overtime to go over every detail of tonight's performance.

"And you liked the way I worked out the beginning of the *soleares?* Where I got up slowly and there was no attention to it?"

Edward took her hand and kissed it as if it were the inside of a fruit.

"To make what is twisted and dry snap like a twig and burn like a log." That had been Bernadette's teacher's favorite way to encourage her. And her favorite story was to tell Bernadette that the greatest dancer she had ever seen, the greatest one in all of Spain, was lame. As he danced with tennis shoes on his feet, *duende,* the soul of the dance, fired through him. No one could take their eyes away.

Bernadette practiced and learned flamenco well. Real flamenco, gypsy flamenco. She began to master the most stylized brand of dancing in the Western world. The most ancient, both noble and debased, display of human experience raised through grace and suffering to something exquisitely dignified. Bernadette had been willing to go full-blown for a moment of *duende,* the life force rising through the body like blood with fire.

*

"What do you mean—he's in love with the way you dance?" Susan's face looked as if it were disassembling. She hadn't arranged this meeting to further understanding. No, she had only hoped to prevent something uncertain and devastating from happening.

Bernadette saw that Susan clutched her purse in her hands and there was a crack in her voice when she said, "Your dancing—that's you, isn't it?"

"No," Bernadette's voice was somber. "It's something beyond me."

Susan squeezed her way past the rim of the table. She had heard enough.

Bernadette didn't respond. Leave him alone? Edward had found her, befriended her, pursued her. And now it was he who said he didn't want to live without her.

When Bernadette left the café, it was shortly after five. She walked past the flamenco theater on Green Street and recalled the first time she had stood timidly in its door. The wild calling of the performers, the wild cheering of the audience. The theater was no more than a hole, dark and murky like a hell. Red and black, garish, strange, close, smelly with foreign cigarettes and women made up to look like whore-saints.

*

A woman and a shadow
are much alike;
on being pursued, they escape;
on being ignored, they follow.

It was past two. The empty streets smelled wet from the fog. Bernadette and Edward walked up Jackson Street into Chinatown.

"Do you want me to drive you home?"

Bernadette looked into Edward's devoted face. "No, I'm very tired now and I need to think before I sleep. I need to think about *soleares* and *siguiriyas.*" She pressed Edward's hand around her arm. "I'm sorry. Maybe tomorrow night we can spend more time. Walk me to Union and then I'll go on alone."

On Columbus, Bernadette made her way towards the bay. Fisherman's Wharf snuggled against the water like a deserted toy town. Alcatraz Island tipped its hat, the Bay Bridge hung like the buttress of a space ship, and the Golden Gate smiled, as it always did, towards Japan.

Bernadette took off her boots and socks and waded into the oil-colored water. Tonight it was true, she had let herself go into the *soleares* as if it were an entire landscape. She had let a force fill up the space between her skin. She, Bernadette Dominica Lee, had vanished for minutes into the atmosphere. Had become nothing. Vacated. She had danced like a shape of air, driven across the stage, back and forth by the breaths of her audience. A dust ball of light. Turned inside out. From the groin reversed. Into nothing. Expired. Yet more consistent with the precision of each step, more exact in her decision to proceed, more related to the degree of rotation in her wrists, to the timing of her feet, than she had ever been. Simultaneously absent and present, the music had driven her out of her body and all those devouring eyes, those strange and unknown faces, had filled her empty tenement.

Where were they going, her and those gawkers who paid their two dollars for a little taste of Spain?

"Bernadette?" The sound whistled out of the darkness. Bernadette turned around. There was no one.

She dipped her hand into the icy bay water and rubbed it on her cheeks. Its coolness soothed the excitement that was still burning inside her.

"Bernadette," and this time all the vowels were extended so that her name went on like a song.

> *A cinnamon angel*
> *watches over your crib,*
> *his head towards the sun,*
> *his feet towards the moon.*

Who said that? Bernadette reeled in a circle. In the darkness the charcoal silhouette of a man stood against the backdrop of the city.

"I used to think flamenco was a bird." The man's voice was graveled with an accent from the East

Coast. Bernadette's eyes squinted at the apparition. "A big, pink bird."

She couldn't see the features on his backlit face, but she could tell he was an unusually small man, a dwarf maybe.

"But then I saw you." It almost sounded like a question. He paused to collect his breath, and an awkward rendition of the *soleares* came out of his mouth. "You never danced like you danced tonight. You know that, don't you?"

Bernadette waded farther north towards the marina. Water surrounded her. She was safe. The moon came out from behind the fog, and the smell of night-blooming jasmine filled the air.

The sound of the dwarf's singing was muffled by the wind off the bay. It was Jerry. Of course, it was him. The goat that plagued them all with his clapping. This was no molester. This was her fan. Her biggest fan.

"I live over there," the shadow of his finger stretched across the sand to the pavement.

Bernadette started to laugh, and as the guttural sound wound up her throat, her entire body shook. Her biggest fan.

"I am a bird," she yelled. "A big, pink bird." And still laughing, Bernadette waded farther away from the tottering man on the shore.

The Rock 'n' Roll Dancer

Baby, you can drive my car
Guess I'm gonna be a star
Baby, you can drive my car
Baaaabbbbeee, I love you

—LENNON / MCCARTNEY

ALTO LIVED in Point Harte, a small town on the coast of Northern California. Point Harte was situated on bluffs that were being gradually eaten away every year by the winter rains. A charming town where tourists congregated in the dry months to walk on the beach and admire the Victorian inns below the bluffs. A town whose indigenous population was almost invisible, whose residents had already retired to lives of art, drugs, trust funds, and country sophistication. It was a busy place, and there was always an odd job for Alto which helped keep fuel in the gas tank and food on the table.

Alto was a capable man, an ardent designer of schemes, a carpenter, a mechanic, a lover, a father, a guitar picker, a deep dreamer, a rock 'n' roll dancer, a boy in a man's body, and a man in a confusing time. He fancied himself a gifted songwriter and, in his increasing moments of self-doubt, claimed that he too could have been a star, a hero of rock 'n' roll. He could have been, but he wasn't.

"I knew 'em all. Jimi, Jerry, Janis. All the ones who caught the glitter that fell on Haight Street. I played with 'em, I got stoned with 'em, I fucked 'em."

When Alto and his first wife left the city to come to Point Harte, they lived in a school bus on a half-acre of land above the ocean. Eventually Alto began to build a home. He hammered, he sawed, he cursed his way through a common room, a kitchen, an indoor bathroom, and a sleeping loft. He salvaged wood, unearthed antique windows and doors, nailed shingles on walls, busted up his picking fingers, sliced open his foot, and lost one of his front teeth. By the time his homemade castle was finished five years later, Alto had two daughters and an imminent divorce. He moved out of his house, across the vegetable garden, and back into the school bus on the bluff.

Those who loved Alto called him talented. Those who resented his free time called him undirected. His parents continued to question how he could live life as if it were a flotation process.

"Yeah," Alto laughed, "how to get higher and higher. Just like my name."

In lucid moments he called his a way to render himself new again in the world. "Like rock 'n' roll," he said. "I'm just looking for a new riff in the songbook of life."

As Alto talked, his fingers strummed across an imaginary guitar, held down a chord for three beats, then skipped up and down the invisible frets like a dragonfly. No one could ever quite figure what Alto meant, but his eagerness made his friends feel fresh and momentarily unencumbered. "I'm going to practice up a little," he said, "get a gig somewhere, up in Mendocino or somewhere, sing my best tunes, dance my best moves."

To listen to Alto was to listen to the repetition of a conversation that had been going on nearly twenty years. And although it was easy to disbelieve him, he made everyone hope he could do just exactly what he said he would. Do it for himself and do it for them too.

"There are signs," he said, "of what I should be doing with my life. Not screwing off making babies and building redwood decks. There are signs that I too should be writing my signature on a dotted line to take millions of rockers into the beat of," and here Alto's preposition always hung off the end of his lips because he could never get to what the power of this love for rock 'n' roll really meant.

"Well, it means youth," he mumbled, drawing lines in the air to show where the equal signs were, "which means hope. And it means sweat, which means sex."

The terms got confused in what Alto wanted to say in the first place because every word that came out of his mouth represented a whole story. "Doesn't it?" And his eyes shifted from his glass of beer to the new acquaintance, who was struggling to follow his circuitry of thoughts.

"All of them, I knew all them when the Avalon and Fillmore were happening." His voice lowered, "They were just a bunch of guys. Regular guys. And suddenly they got to be heroes or something."

Alto's left fingers bent back and forth across his waist in scales. He flipped his thumb up to Joey to signal him for another beer.

"Once, a couple of years after I moved out here, I was going over the mountain." And he meant traveling from San Francisco north around the green winter bonnet of Mount Tamalpais. "And see, it was raining, and I was standing there in the dark with my thumb out, and everything was so black, and well."

"Alto, we've heard this one," Joey said, sliding the glass of tap down the bar.

"See," Alto turned back to the stranger, "a car finally stopped, and the driver opened the door. I climbed onto the seat of his old Dodge." Alto's hands, both of them, lifted and faced each other like a plaster statue in prayer. "I said, 'Thanks' to the driver, and he said, 'Bad night' to me. And then I saw who it was."

When Alto had first begun to tell this story, it was Bob Dylan or maybe John Lennon driving, but lately he had substituted Boss Bruce.

"When I climbed out of the Dodge and looked into the driver's eyes looking back, then I knew that it meant I had to go and do it—do what Mick had done." Alto threw his head back and laughed a sound that resembled a snort. "I've been trying to figure out how ever since."

That was Alto's cue. As soon as he finished his story about hitchhiking over Mount Tam and running into Eric Clapton, he staggered off to his car.

"Night, Alto."

"Night, Joey."

Alto leaned back in the driver's seat. He rubbed the surface of the steering wheel like his favorite part of a woman. He turned on the ignition and let it idle. He tuned the radio to his favorite station. It was playing Cream. Alto could feel everything inside him quickening. He closed his eyes and imagined driving to Ruby's Club outside Novato. The music from inside the club was seething. Parts of Alto's body were hot, parts of his head too. Cream turned into Little Richard. That was better. That was rock 'n' roll. Alto clutched the steering wheel like the arm of a girl. He moved it around the dance floor in his mind as if they'd been dancing together for years. He drove her across the floor of Ruby's and dipped her back towards the floor in a motion that resembled a chrome bumper.

The next song on the radio was "California Dreamin'" and Alto thought, "If I hear that goddamn song once more, I'm gonna puke." He turned off the radio, jerked the stick shift into second, and roared up to the bluff overlooking the ocean.

Now there were three children—two older girls and a baby boy. His second wife lived with him in the school bus above Point Harte. And the first wife lived in the homemade house across the garden with a second husband and their twin sons.

Alto was building an addition to the school bus to extend its rear door out like a glass wing. He planned to leave earth for the floor of the entry and plant grass for a rug. Above the greenhouse would be his sanctuary for writing songs, playing his guitar, and getting high. And along with Alto's blueprint of a new improved school bus were the photographs and documentary films of him, Alto Stratacaster, primo rock 'n' roll maker, propped up against a boulder over the edge of the world playing his amplified brains out.

"Drunk on dreams," the first wife scowled at the second. "I still can't stand it."

The second wife tried to demonstrate her loyalty, "All he needs is plain moral support and a little encouragement."

"You'll see. You're gonna need more than that pretty soon. You're gonna need plain food. The baby's gonna need plain milk."

All around, tasks begged Alto to get them done. Wood was needed for the stove in the school bus, the teenage girls wanted help on their homework, his second wife had to get to town, the husband of the first wife was hoping Alto would play pool.

Alto was busy, and nothing could move him from beneath his headphones.

"Dinner's ready."

"Not hungry."

"Baby's crying."

"Huh?"

"Honey, can't you pick up the baby?"

For days Alto sat, dancing to the unpressed songs spinning in his mind.

"Then tell him to go out and do it," the first wife told the second. "Maybe Joey would hire him to play on Saturday night."

"Don't you see he can't? He loves the music, but he hates all the other stuff."

"Yeah, yeah," Alto said, "yeah." He had the second verse down and it was beautiful. "Yeah, rock 'n' roll," and this time he was speaking to the motion of the sea below the bluff, "is something to love and perpetuate. A force to give into, a magnet and a void."

Something to love. "And it never talks back," Alto looked across the bar at Joey.

Never argued like his wives, whined like his daughters, cried like his baby boy, yelped like his dogs, went to seed like his garden. It was a love that appeared and disappeared in air from the pressure of his fingers on metal strings, that reappeared on the radio and record player, in cars and bars, in private listening, or in public with thousands and thousands of dancers stretching the limits of their skin to climb into the music. And although it could sound like the worst – dirty, loud, even criminal – it always reminded Alto of what was the best – spontaneous, assured, and brave.

Once Alto moved outside his earphones, he was elated.

"I got it now, honey. I got this one all worked out."

He made lists of his tunes, bought new sets of strings for his guitar. He was smiling all the time. And crazed with business. In two days he finished the walls on the school bus addition, harvested his marijuana, changed his son's diapers, helped his daughters with algebra. He was getting ready, making certain everyone would be able to go on without him when he went out on the road. He was jamming the music in his head and through his fingers. Jamming so hard they bled.

After fifteen days of solid preparation, Alto stopped. Stopped the way he always had before. He yelled through the open window of the school bus to the ocean and its audience of sea life, "Nothing's ever going to happen with all this! Nothing's ever going to happen with me!"

And the repetition of the word *nothing* clouded over the glass. The sweat on his palms was acrid from the riffs that jumped from fret to fret, over and over. Nothing. Nothing but a fool's spell. And he licked the blood and wiped the sweat through his hair. His large hands lifted the guitar and swung it around his head like a slingshot. He whirled with it through the door of the school bus, down to the edge of the bluff. He ran around in circles, looking like the shadow of a dog in agony. A black lab with porcupine quills in his muzzle. Howling.

Alto turned and cursed every chore around him, and his curses sang out in short ejaculations of spit, going over the edge into the ocean. And finally after every name of every boss, wife, child, parent, and teacher was hosted with his maledictions, he ceased. He fell down on the dark grass and crawled back on his knees to the school bus to smoke a joint and cry himself to sleep.

The First Dancer

To speak of it is to speak of everything. When we walked along the edges of the river, following the waters upstream and downstream, back and forth to the sea, through the seasons, we swayed on our feet, tipping our reflections out from the cool banks down the slopes to the water.

Under the shadows of the trees, we used our eyes, looking for enemy and friend. We walked with our noses and our sense of touch. Dancing, we ran, and the children skipped. We used our ears to listen for comforting or dangerous alterations in temperature, in wind, in the sounds of the forest. The number of birds and the loudness of their singing drew our attention from one side of the river to the other. Their voices mingled with the activities of all the other creatures, including our own, chipping stone, cutting reed, digging roots, comforting the young and aged.

Our voices were as numerous as the thousand stars that poured out into the blackness once we rolled away from our source of light. Then a softer and paler source would appear and surprise us with caprices of its shape, or run away from us altogether into the smoky and opaque night. We slept in the darkness, and we danced with the moon.

To speak of it is misleading, for we had few ways to describe it in words.

Everyday we rose, bathed, we broke our fast, and walked out from our shelter to look for food. Our walking day dance was first of all to find nourishment. Our callused hands shoveled the mosses and long grass that protected the underground things we liked to eat. We beat into the earth with our hands, our feet. We used our voices to pass the time, inventing words for our new discoveries.

The children gathered stones and sticks for games in the mud and sand as we cut stalks, picked berries, dried fruit. The world of the forest, the meadows, and the sea, the attire of the changing plant life all around us were our inspiration for poetry. The signs of the animals, their walks, their postures, their flights, we made into dance.

Obviously, we came to discern the changes of cycles, through the days and the seasons and the years. Our food supply, our means of shelter, and the protection of our bodies from the biting winds that drove up out of the big sea forced us to anticipate signals of change. We counted on many of the animals around to remind us of these signs. Once we began to consciously relay the information about such matters to each other, we could take moments to relax, even better organize the tasks of work. As a result, our minds were allowed to wander, and the children were left to play. We let the smells in the air warn and recall to us the shape of cycles, so that we became not only familiar but unsurprised by many of the events that constantly affected our lives.

To speak of it is to shred its mightiness into little facts.

Our observation of the night skies only confirmed the repetition of patterns. Light and dark, hot and cold. We remembered how the stars changed. In that way we were able to dance in particular directions. North, east, south, west. And then lay our heads to rest and receive the messages of dreams.

Every event offered us an occasion to worship. Each birth, each death. They were incessant. Unions between mates. Dry times and plentiful times. Forest fires, unusual birds, thunder, self-perpetuating orchards, and ordinary as well as extraordinary celestial variations. Celebrations for everything gave us the occasion to put our bodies together in a jumble and dance a prayer that we would continue to survive.

Then, more of us would die, many perhaps, and more of us get born, fewer perhaps. Young ones would grow older and some very few would survive to have winter hair on their head, and like that, we would continue our lives, dancing along the river, digging for roots in the ground.

The Ballroom Dancer

"WHAT'S THE DIFFERENCE between a ball and a prom?" Cynthia slipped into the front seat next to her dad.

"I don't know exactly." Hugh paused thoughtfully, flicking the end of his cigarette into the gravel while the car warmed up.

Cynthia waited patiently, as she always did, for him to answer her question. She knew he eventually would.

"Well, a ball, well, it's a big, formal thing. Everyone comes in limousines, and there's a butler standing at the top of a stairs that leads down into the actual ballroom. He's there to announce the names of the guests. There are only adults at a ball, and they're all wearing tuxedos, furs, jewels, and long, expensive gowns. And they aren't ordinary people. They're queens, presidents, dukes, movie stars. I'm not sure if anyone has a good time, but everyone is very glad to be invited."

"And a prom?" Cynthia knew she was going to be disappointed.

"A prom is almost like that, but it's for kids, for high school and college kids."

"Have you ever been to a ball?"

Hugh's eyes assumed a distance and he lit another cigarette. They had reached the highway, and he was on the lookout for danger. Squirrels, dogs, possums, horses, cats, and the occasional stray cow. Any of the wild or domesticated animals that moved around in abundance out in the country, wandering alone, either wild, lost, bewildered, or mad.

"In college the big dances were almost like balls. We dressed up, we rented penguin suits, we bought corsages for the girls, we polished our cars. We thought we were princes." He smiled his wide, handsome smile at his daughter. She still thought he was one.

"And is that where you met Momma?"

Cynthia's parents were in the middle of their seventeenth year of marriage and the seventh month of their divorce. They had been separated from each other even longer, but the state of North Carolina wouldn't accept the final dissolution of their marriage until a year had elapsed.

"No, I met her in the dentist's office. You know the story."

"But you took her to balls? You did, didn't you?"

Hugh winced at the memory of carrying Lynn, Cynthia's mother, out to the parking lot to throw up. Lynn always drank too much, danced too fast, laughed too loud. Slugging down shots of Jack Daniels to keep up with him.

"And you remember what she wore, don't you?"

"'She wore blue velvet.'" Hugh hummed his old favorite. "'Bluer than velvet was the night.' Lynn usually chose dark colors to match her hair and eyes."

Cynthia persisted. "And what kind of flowers did you bring her?"

"Fat, ugly orchids, Cindy. Let's not keep talking about this. That was then. Okay, honey? This is now."

Cynthia settled back into the deluxe passenger seat of her daddy's Lincoln. She closed her eyes and chewed her bottom lip with her teeth, rolling little balls of skin between her braces.

"Let's talk about your prom, honey. That's what really counts today. Are there any boys you like?"

"A couple." Cynthia sighed. "But I don't have a boyfriend. They aren't boyfriends." One of them spoke to her only when he needed his French assignment.

She swung her lanky arm across the dash to take a swallow of the Coke inside the magnetic coaster. The interior of her daddy's car always smelled like his cologne. It smelled like sailboats in moonlight, convertibles in the wind, ski lodges, tropical islands, the romantic kinds of places where girls meet boys and women meet men. She hoped the boys she danced with at the prom would remember to wear cologne, even if they didn't shave.

"Besides, they're both in the twelfth grade. Can I change the station?"

Cynthia fiddled with the knobs. It wasn't easy to get good reception on the winding mountain roads, and the only thing that ever came in clearly was the news. Cynthia tried to imagine how the dark gymnasium

would feel, how the lights in the rafters would spotlight her, how her circle of friends would turn
around in unison, "Cindy, we've been waiting for
you. I love your dress, your hair, your shoes."

Then the music would start up, but Cynthia
wouldn't look around to see who was going to ask her
to dance. She would pause until someone, someone
who didn't even go to her school—Owen's cousin
from Rhode Island or Jimmy Burrow's stepbrother
from Raleigh—tapped her shoulder and said, "You're
Cynthia Buchanan, aren't you?"

"Yes," her eyes held his gaze.

"Could I?"

"Yes." By this time her eyes had looked away and
she had slipped her hand into his.

Cynthia stared at the distant silhouette of mountains. She didn't care if her parents were getting a
divorce. Everybody could feel badly about it. If her
friends wanted to sympathize or if they thought she
was brave, that was all right. If the adults thought she
was mature, that was all right too. One way or the
other, she had decided she didn't care.

In fact, it was a relief to live without the noise of
her parents' fights, the loud accusations, the bruises
on her mother's arms that she watched fading from
blue to yellow. Bruises, Lynn said, she got from falling
down, but were obviously from the battles that went
on in the bedroom, the kitchen, the basement, wher-
ever her parents unluckily met, after one or both of
them had had too much to drink.

"I don't need for them to be together," she told
herself. She simply needed the assurance that she

would be able to carry on her own life. Have their permission, their benediction to go out on dates, to dances and restaurants, to movies and ski resorts, sail to tropical islands, travel to fraternity parties at distant colleges. Carry on the future that loomed romantically towards her from the adult world. Cynthia's only wish was to forget that her parents were at the disastrous end of that cycle. Forget the divorce that acknowledged the defeated promise of her own seventeenth year.

"Let's stop and get some lunch," Hugh pulled into the parking lot of a small diner.

Cynthia knew this mountain road by heart, as it wound down the passes from the Smokies into the Appalachian foothills and over to Atlanta. She had taken this drive once a month since she was a little girl. She went to Atlanta to see doctors, visit her grandparents, and go shopping.

Cynthia was of the opinion that Atlanta was the place where special things existed – large restaurants whose menus were written in foreign languages, store windows so beautiful they made her want to live in them, movie theaters that looked like Moorish castles. Among her friends she was the only one who had eaten French and Chinese and Italian and Japanese food. Cynthia's girlfriends envied her cosmopolitan opportunities, and Cynthia had her own small superior feelings. She realized that although it didn't matter now if she knew what *escargots* were, she guessed that someday it would mean something. Someday it would reflect not only who she was, but who she loved.

"Daddy, we're going to have to buy shoes and leave them off in Buckhead to be dyed to match my dress. Momma said she'll pick them up on Friday when she comes down."

"What's she going to Atlanta for?" Hugh tried to sound casual, mildly curious, in fact disinterested, but his voice rasped through his BLT.

Hugh's mind reeled back to the fraternity party where he found Lynn in the backseat with George Gunney. Drunken bitch. Never able to hold her liquor or keep her hands to herself. He had given her his fraternity pin—the slut—two diamonds, two rubies, one pearl. And he had loved the way it rode on the crest of her tit, especially in a lambswool sweater. He had loved it until the time she wobbled suspiciously through the back door of the Phi Delt house with the pin on the inside, underneath the sweater, inside out as if she had been redressing in the yard. And then that bird dog George came through the same door five minutes later. Hugh tucked in his breath through the next bite. That woman could have driven him to choke to death.

"You know, Cindy, you're a real beauty. I know just how it's going to feel to see you at the dance."

Cynthia looked at her father with idolatrous appreciation. She hoped there was another one like him around, with just a little more blond in his hair, please, and a little less temper.

"And today we're gonna find a dress almost as beautiful as you."

Next to trout fishing, Hugh's second favorite pleasure was driving his daughter from wish to wish. He was a man who loved to buy for the people he cherished. There wasn't any other way he knew how to express his devotion. When that simple connection with his wife Lynn had shorted out and she had come to refuse his gifts along with his affection, he was helpless.

Two years ago Lynn had made the declaration that she wanted a "meaningful relationship, not things." Hugh didn't have a clue as to what that meant. He thought his personality alone made his relationships meaningful, and he had always been told he had a good one. He had never considered it differently. Frankly, he couldn't. If he was able to get along and tell a story well and drink it up with his friends and make enough money to buy most anything he wanted, then that was charm enough for a lifetime. It wasn't polite to have personal and unique feelings, especially if they might interfere with a good personality.

"Was Momma the prettiest girl you knew?"

The road had now widened into a freeway, three empty lanes heading southeast into Atlanta.

"You know that picture of you and Momma at the fall rush party? She has on a dark green dress. It's the color of a pine forest. And her hair's done up. There's a flower in her hair. Remember, Daddy? Momma told me to look for something crepe or chiffon."

Cynthia's voice trailed off into the soft shoulders along the side of the road. She loved studying the photos of her parents, leaning into each other, squashed among their gang of friends, frosted mugs of beer and pewter goblets of bourbon raised to the tall white columns of the Phi Delt house. Always smiling. In the pictures they were always smiling.

Cynthia knew some of the other people in the photos too. Her dad's cousin, Freddie. Everyone called him Lunch, but her daddy would never tell her why. He was there with his future wife, Janette. Cousin Freddie had been killed in an Air Force transport accident. Her mother's sister was in one of the pictures. She lived over in Charlotte with three kids and a husband who inherited a lot of money and rode around in his airplane all day.

Cynthia tried to wring some clue from the photographs of what it was like to be twenty, twenty-one, twenty-two. In those split seconds of time she hoped to catch a hint as to who might be holding her someday. What kind of body, or what combination of shoes, haircut, shirt might also affix her to the lineage of marriage, love, and history.

When shopping for his daughter, Hugh preferred to go to Saks Fifth Avenue. The selection was small but choice, the location convenient. Saks was situated in one of Atlanta's exclusive Northwest shopping malls, near a bar that Hugh always had good luck at when he was in Atlanta alone.

Cynthia and her father caught the elevator to the second floor. Cynthia had just moved from pre-teen to junior. Stepping from one patterned carpet to the next, they found themselves surrounded by young mannequins dressed in tennis wear. Off to the left was the bridal department, filled with yards of white organza and tulle. Off to the right was sportswear.

"We want to see the formals." Hugh said authoritatively. He always sounded so certain. Cynthia liked that.

The saleswoman led them into a small oval salon. The walls were finished in pale blue, and French Provincial chairs were arranged in a semicircle in front of the mirrors. "Did you have anything particular in mind?"

"She's going to her first prom," Hugh smiled.

Cynthia stared at the saleswoman's neck. Two orange rings of powder streaked around it like the tail of a comet.

The saleswoman pulled hangers of gowns off the rack and hung them where Hugh and Cynthia were seated.

There were five pastels to try. Cynthia followed the saleswoman to the entrance of the dressing room. There she carefully, preciously lifted the first dress. She checked the price tag and undid the zipper, slipping the salmon-layered chiffon over her padded bra and panties. Then she floated out of the dressing room, walking softly in her bare feet, already feeling the moonlight engulf her.

Hugh made an enthusiastic gesture for each of the dresses, but they all concurred that the salmon chiffon was the right choice.

Confidently holding her dress box, Cynthia stopped to look at the gloves. She chose a pair of thick white cotton ones embroidered in clusters of French knots across the back of the hand. At the hosiery counter she chose pale salmon stockings. At accessories she found two pearl barrettes for her hair and a long, cream-colored silk scarf to go with her mother's fur stole.

With each purchase, Hugh was lavishly kissed and adored. He was willing to go on buying all afternoon.

Finally, after some new underwear and a nightie, it was time to drive home.

Every evening for the next week Cynthia practiced dancing with her mother Lynn. Lynn guided her through the box step and the cha-cha-cha.

"You've got it, honey."

"Momma, we don't do those dances. If it's a fast dance, nobody touches anybody. And if it's slow," Cynthia flung her body into her mother's arms and gripped her neck like a python, "you have to know someone pretty well."

Lynn put on Herb Alpert and the Tijuana Brass. She took Cynthia's hands in hers and pumped her arms up and down like levers, moving backwards across the carpet, drawing Cynthia towards her. "It's fun, isn't it? It's the calypso. Now you can teach him how to do it."

"Him who?" Cynthia asked suspiciously.

"You tell me when you meet him."

On the Friday of the prom, Cynthia came home from school to begin. First, she washed her hair and rolled it on giant bristled curlers. With the cap dryer on her head, she worked on her nails. Then she took a bubble bath and rubbed herself with perfumed powder.

"Dinner's ready," Lynn called through the bathroom door.

Cynthia stepped out of her tile palace. She touched the rollers on her head. "I can't eat, Momma. I can't even think about eating."

"Your father called. He wants to bring you home after the prom. He wants you to spend the night at his house." Lynn tried to sound cheerful. "I said I'd have to ask you."

Lynn would have preferred to exclude Hugh from the evening. She hated sharing their daughter. Especially this moment when Cynthia was so pleased, so expectant about the promises of men. Lynn also hated the idea of Hugh taking Cindy back to his place afterwards. To his apartment, where all sorts of women came and went with their own personal keys. That's what the private detective had discovered, and that's what Lynn planned to bring out in court if there was any question about her having full custody. She hoped she had the chance to tell the judge that Hugh Buchanan had a string of ponies that spanned the entire Smoky Mountain chain.

Cynthia went back to the bathroom. She didn't want her mother to see her again until she was completely dressed.

"Mommmmma," Cindy's voice was a long wail. "I'm ready."

Lynn sat stiffly in the living room, watching the door of her daughter's bedroom open. Cynthia walked slowly, ceremonially through it like silk tissue. Her dress, her shiny chestnut hair, her skin and lips, her willowed outline wrapped in a chiffon pastry shell.

Lynn's exclamation stopped in her throat. The image before her swept her back to fraternity parties, college dances, country clubs, ski weeks, beach houses, events that once filled every weekend in her life. Her own closet full of silk dresses, scrapbooks pressed with corsages, matchbook souvenirs from expensive restaurants, a collection of gifts, two fraternity pins, one sweetheart lavaliere. Her first lessons in smoking menthol, french kissing, chugalugging beer. There she was, herself before her, raised up in her own image.

"God!" Lynn yelled it, "You look beautiful. You really do. Hey, hold it right there." Lynn ran for the Polaroid. "Don't move."

Cynthia slipped on her mother's rabbit stole. They drove down the hill to pick up Cynthia's girlfriend, then swung through the small town back over to the high school. Lynn pulled into the horseshoe drive by the gym.

The girls slipped quickly out of the car and away into their world, gliding towards the gaping black entry of the school. The first sounds of the band rushed out into the night. Clusters of students hung by the door. A million stars sprinkled the sky.

"Cindy, come here a minute," Lynn called. Cynthia groaned. This was going to ruin her entrance.

"I just wanted to tell you that I love you."

Cynthia's smile was tolerant. "Oh, Momma." She sprinted back to her friends. Lynn watched Cynthia hesitate to go in, watched her question what the preparation for this evening—the dress, the gloves, the stockings, the fur—actually meant. Did it mean she would really fall in love? Did it mean someone would really fall in love with her? Lynn wondered how many years it would take her daughter to discover those weren't the only two questions in the universe. Lynn wanted to shout out to her, "Those aren't the only questions in the universe."

Lynn drove back through the town she had lived in since her marriage. It was home now. A small town in the mountains of North Carolina. There wasn't a word she was permitted to say about what had happened to love in her lifetime. There was nothing short of cynical, bitter, or mean that would allow her to break the spell that the songs, the television, the Constitution had promised her daughter. Everything promised her love, and was her own mother going to tell her it was different?

Three hours later – a lifetime – Cynthia stood again outside the gymnasium door, watching as her friends climbed into their parents' cars. She looked up at the stars, the millions and millions of stars that littered the mountain sky. How was it that no matter how much you thought something was going to be like something, it never was? How come that was always, always, always true? And her father was late of all nights, and now she was the only one left on the curb outside the school.

The band members wheeled their equipment down the cement ramp.

"You looked lovely tonight, Cindy. Did you have a good time?"

"Thank you, Mrs. Weston. See you on Monday."

A dread spread over Cynthia, and she blushed in the dark. Her parents were getting divorced. Her parents were getting divorced. The phrase repeated itself over and over until it screamed in her head. I am beautiful because everyone tells me over and over, and my parents are getting divorced. I went to the dance tonight, I went to the dance tonight, and my daddy is late. My daddy is late, damn him. And my parents are getting divorced. She watched the quadruple headlights of Hugh's car turn into the drive.

"Cindy, I'm sorry. I was really trying to make it on time."

Cynthia slid into the front seat like a piece of ice. She didn't say hello. She didn't say anything. She was cold from standing out in the night air.

"I want to take you over to Highlands for a midnight cherry Coke. How about it? We'll drive up the high road and look over the mountaintops to Tennessee. Forgive me, honey. You really look like something."

Cynthia swallowed. She waited for her father's inevitable questions.

"Was the dance fun?" Hugh pulled a cigarette out of the pack and pushed in the lighter. "Did you have a good time?"

Cynthia could smell the strong odor of liquor on his breath. It was a smell that accompanied moonlight sails to Caribbean islands. Cynthia's lips pushed against each other. She was trying not to cry. "I didn't dance."

"Not once?"

"Not one dance," she said defiantly.

"You mean nobody asked you to dance?" Hugh's breath drew on his cigarette, and his voice raced ahead. "They were scared, honey. You know boys are really scared of girls. I was. Nobody knew it, but I was. Your mother, she thought I was a prince, that I held the world in my hand, that I wasn't scared of anything. How could I be scared of a girl when I went out every Saturday and faced a lineup of animals on a football field? But I'm telling you, those boys were scared."

Hugh patted the top of his daughter's gloved hand. "You looked so pretty, honey, you scared them off. That's what happened. They just couldn't bring themselves to ask you."

"They asked me to dance, Daddy."

Hugh's fingers rubbed across the skin of his daughter's bare arm.

"But they were all losers," Cynthia said emphatically.

"Losers, honey, what's a loser? Honey, you gotta give somebody a chance."

"You may not know what one is, but I know."

Hugh looked at Cynthia's profile. In the dark, she looked just like her mother, her dark hair falling softly like a mantle around her shoulders, her alabaster skin shining like moonlight itself. For an instant Hugh didn't know whether he loved or hated her.

"I promised Momma I would never dance with a loser. Momma said, 'Cindy, it's more fun to stand with your friends than go out there and dance with someone you could never care for and who could never care for you.' It's true, Daddy, I'd rather stand with my friends the whole night than dance with a loser. 'Never again,' Momma says, 'never again.'"

The lights of the town blinked madly between Cynthia's eyes and the windshield of the car. Hugh pressed his foot on the accelerator down to the floor. That bitch. Cynthia lurched against the seat. That bitch.

The African Dancer

SONNY GLIDED BAREFOOT down the street. Her long skirt brushed the leaves on the sidewalk, her dozens of tiny blond braids reflected the sun. On her back she balanced a woven African basket in which her small mulatto son, Yacuba, sat upright.

As Sonny walked along, she swung the baby from side to side with a slow hip stride and played her bamboo flute. Yacuba poked his head out of the wide opening and pulled on one of his mother's beaded braids.

"Stop, Yacuba."

Yacuba tugged Sonny's hair.

"That hurt me. You want me to pull your hair?"

Sonny raised her voice from a reprimand to a threat, "Stop it." Her voice combined the accent of a white suburban education with the experience of a city ghetto.

Yacuba's hand slid back inside the basket. He stared at the trees sailing over his head and listened to his mother's flute. He swayed and swayed.

La, la, la, do, la, la.

By the time Sonny reached the dance studio, Yacuba was asleep, his head resting across Sonny's shoulder.

Hush, little baby, don't you cry.
Don't you know your momma was born to die?

Sonny sang softly as she shifted the basket from her back to the floor and unwound the batik sarong from her waist to lay across the couch. She placed Yacuba on top of the material and covered him with the padding in the bottom of the basket.

The River Jordan is muddy and cold.
Chills the body but not the soul.

Two drummers had arrived in the studio.
Whap.
Yacuba wouldn't wake up, no matter how loud.
Whap. Whap, wha, wha, whap.
Baby was conceived on drum music, and Sonny amazed her class by dancing through her entire pregnancy. Yes, sisters, yes. As soon as Yacuba was two weeks old, she was back in the studio.
Whap. Whap.
Eddie beat his pewter-colored palms against the resonating hide of the congas.
Whap. Wha, wha, wha, whap.
Instantly, Sonny felt herself ready to dance. In fact, she had already started, as if it were the most natural part of her day, moving slowly in small shuffles from Yacuba to the large circular dance floor. Moving as if

pieces of her body were ignited by the sound. Arms, legs, fingers, wrists. Shoulders, knees, neck, chest. Deep into the interior of her abdomen, up to her heart, out to the skin itself. As Eddie's hands banged across the hides, Sonny's skin woke up. Hearts beat better to sounds like that.

Whap. Wha, wha, wha, whap.

The vibrations of the congas skipped across the room, leaping like a flat stone over a lake's surface. No one could stand still with the infusion of such sounds. It was as powerful as loud electric rock, but pre-electric, prehistoric, speaking the first universal language. The drums beckoned, implored, commanded the body to communicate first to them, and then to whomever was nearby.

Whap. Wha, wha, wha, wha, wha, whap.

The other dancers enlarged their circle to make a place for Sonny. The women stood, swaying slowly with their bodies—bronze, coffee, black, and white. Their strong legs bare, their leotards already showing stains of perspiration from the heat in the room, the heat in the rhythm, the equatorial heat that the sounds recalled.

These women had known Sonny a long time. As black African dancers, they had seen many white girls come to their dance studio in Oakland. Sonny was different. She not only stayed, she swayed and sweated, ate and laughed with them. She was a friend, mother of a black man's child. Yes, a sister. Exactly what Sonny longed to be.

In the back was a group of children who belonged to the women. They were there to watch or clap or play with each other in the makeshift nursery where Yacuba now lay sleeping. The children came no matter what else was happening because their mothers came. It was a ritualized part of their lives too. And priorities at home put dancing at the top.

Sonny's teacher, Aisha, walked briskly in a circle around the other dancers. Aisha walked fast, in time with the drums.

Immediately, the dancers mimicked her in a circle of their own. Then Aisha shifted to a series of simple steps, a combination of one jump, two running strides, and a turn. The ring of dancers watched her and followed. Gradually, as they warmed up together, the dancers began to sense Aisha's change of movement. By the end of the first set, all of them were shifting positions, alternating arms and feet, moving their chests, buttocks, abdomens simultaneously.

Aisha stepped back and yelled *siku,* the word for "day" in the African language Swahili. The others repeated it, including Eddie and the drummers.

Siku! Siku!

Each time, the sound was louder. Then Aisha shouted the word for "night," indicating that after one group said *siku,* the other should answer with *giza.*

Siku! Giza!

Siku! Giza!

Greeting for greeting.

The dancers watched Aisha's motions as she depicted an African story in dance. She crouched like the hunter, she hid like the hunted, she rolled her hips around in celebration of the kill. The beat of the drums and the pace of the steps got faster and faster.

The others followed. They crouched like the hunter, they hid like the hunted, they rolled their hips around in celebration of the kill.

Whap. Wha, wha, wha, whap.

The circle moved around and around. The feet of the dancers made thuds that syncopated with the drums. Their chests moved like bellows. Their bottoms arched, their bellies contracted. And their sleek hands lifted as far as their arms would carry them – to the ceiling, the roof, on to the heavens – matching this celebration of matter as it moved from energy into spirit.

Aisha raised her head to Eddie and the drums stopped. The dancers fell down on their spot, exhausted and exhilarated. Then Aisha started the story again.

This time the dancers planted crops, swinging their bodies like sickles across the floor.

Whap. Wha, wha, wha, whap.

In celebration of the harvest. One plunge to the inside right, three fast shuffles, a moving turn, shoulder shimmy to the outside, three more shuffles, a low-crouched jump forward and back. Up down on the feet, deep into the knees, the dancers kept going until the drums, the walls, the floor receded into one continuous sensation of heat. Distinctions faded to reverberations. And revelation of what African tribal dance was about surfaced through an exhausted, unanimous surrender.

Sonny was wet, soaked, but still ready to keep going. She hated to stop, to let go of the sensations pouring through her body. It was always unnatural when class actually ended, as if their experience were something that could be regulated by the clock. As if the dancing were something that could be determined by a schedule.

Sonny tried – every time she tried – to take the feelings of the dance home with her, back out into the street. Feelings that were testimonies to the powers of her senses. She wanted more than anything to sustain an awareness that did not depend on intellect or race or economy. That depended instead on her nature, first as animal, and then as primitive human.

Whap. Wha, wha, wha, whap.

Sonny stayed over on a large, well-lit avenue that ran from affluent North Oakland across 51st Street into the mixed neighborhood where she lived. Meaning, by mixed, that there were addicts and nonaddicts, pimps and nonpimps, whores and nonwhores, mostly poor and unemployed blacks.

Everyone on her block was a renter, and that meant that someone was always moving in or out. It meant that the police cruised her block once an hour. It also meant that families were evicted with nowhere to go. And that drug deals went down at noon. And that the yards, back and front, were common ground for anyone running. And that every single window within a ten-mile radius had bars on it.

Sonny had lived on this street ever since she arrived in California eight years before. She came straight to Oakland and never once considered living next door in prestigious Berkeley. No, she headed directly to the home of the Black Panthers, and even though they had vacated, she still carried their pride.

On her own street she had seen crime. She had witnessed deep abuse – outrageous acts between men and women, women and children, children and dogs. She herself had almost been raped, then rescued, then ripped off like everyone else. Taken to church by her neighbors, taught to cook Southern and rural and black by her neighbors, adopted collards as the vegetable of choice. Slept with two men in her bed, both black – one now dead, the other in prison. She had had Yacuba in the hospital down the way, deeper into Oakland, where the sirens always had a reason to sound. And after Yacuba's birth, welcomed her parents to her home, the first time they had ever visited. They promised to help if she'd come home with them. Instead, Sonny took a part-time job at the Italian deli. When she wasn't working, she was at home with Yacuba or at the community dance center.

Whap. Wha, wha, wha, whap.

All her life, Sonny's battles had been identified by the headlines concerning people of color. At the age of nine she saw black children attacked and beaten by an Alabama mob.

Whap.

During the civil rights movement, Sonny fixed on the plight of blacks in the North and South. Encouraged by her Quaker family, she grew up with causes that always belonged to someone somewhere else. When she was older and learned about the militant Panthers, a group of blacks in Oakland that weren't afraid to stand up, she felt her time had come to join the Third World. Oakland was about as close as she could get without a passport.

Sonny came to California to stand up. Those were even her words. And everything that was important to her standing had happened in Oakland. She had discarded the hopes of her parents to become a professional, a doctor like her father, a nurse like her sister. Or to marry a peer—"a white liberal," she sneered. She had left behind the possibility of perpetuating her parents' lives, their position, even their causes, which now appeared weak or safe. There was no risk involved for what they believed. And recently they had retired, meaning they had shut themselves away in a planned, safe, locked community out of fear of exactly what Sonny chose to live among.

Whap. Whap. Wha, wha, wha, whap.

Sonny had met Aisha and the sisters in Oakland. When she first started to dance, she was tentative and awkward.

"Come on, girl." Aisha pointed to her in class early on. "Get down on those haunches and stick out that fanny. You can do it. I know you can do it."

Wha, wha, wha, whap.

In the dancing Sonny had discovered a passion which encompassed everything—her body, her politics, her style of expression, and after Yacuba's birth, even her motherhood.

She joined with groups in Oakland to free people from prison, to campaign against police abuse, to educate herself and anyone else about organizing against injustice. She adopted a black accent, a black hairstyle, and an impatience for anyone who didn't recognize the color of her sincerity. These were the ways she made herself more believable to herself.

Maybe more accurately, she was a black person born in a white skin. And beaded collars, dashikis, and talking drums were as much a homecoming for her as her brown neighbors. Their cause was her cause because she was them. White always, blond maybe, but inside something else.

"I've become a student of African dance," she wrote to her sister in Pennsylvania. Her sister never wrote back.

Whap. Wha, wha, wha.

Sonny had volunteered to organize a visit to San Bruno County Jail. To mail the names, social security numbers, current addresses, and birth dates for the dancers and drummers to Ralph, the jail's recreation director. Aisha had set up permission with Ralph to come and dance for the female inmates and, if it worked out, conduct regular dance workshops at the jail. Getting security clearance for everyone was the first step.

Generally at San Bruno, prisoners were either black or Hispanic. They had committed misdemeanors—petty theft, prostitution, failure-to-appear. Many were officially sedated for their stay—depressed, lethargic, sullen.

Ralph met the dancers and drummers at the guardhouse. "I want to remind you that when you leave, these girls don't leave with you. They have to stay. And we have to stay with them. I'm not telling you what you can and cannot say, what you can and cannot do. But if they get too excited, then we all have to pay for their entertainment the hard way."

Sonny looked at the faces of the other dancers.

Whap.

After all, what did this Ralph know about women? Black women? Women who had to sell themselves to see their way clear? Women whose own men, husbands had forced them into the streets? Supplied them with drugs. Given them babies and left. "Who was the real criminal?" Sonny wanted to scream. He could talk from his self-important directorship of recreation. Whap.

The gate of the jail opened, and the van drove behind the wired fences towards the smaller of two concrete facilities. Through the kitchen and large dining hall, the troupe filed into the living room. The lime-sherbet walls were covered with the remnants of graffiti. On one side of the room were a couple of crumbling sofas, a television, two dozen folding chairs. On the other side were several small barred windows. At the same time the dancers entered, thirty inmates filed through a thick metal door.

"Hey, sister. Hey, pretty sister. You got some stuff, sister?"

"Aw, shut up, bitch. Shut your big mouth."

"Girlie, you lookin' good."

"Hey, hot blood. Hey, you with the arms." The drummers looked down at the floor. "Hey, you with the drum, I'm talking to you."

"Whooeee girlie. Will you hush?"

Sonny looked down too. At her light freckled hands, her long opal fingernails. "Jail," and she could almost feel that this was where she was supposed to be. This was really where the suffering was happening.

Whap. Wha, wha, wha. Whap. Whap.

The drummers had started to play softly. Two inmates, who had already been told to sit in their chairs and behave, were jumping and hollering like they had just been dosed with speed. They were in their seats now, but they were moving at the same time.

Ralph raised his fingers in a V to signal quiet. "You are expected to sit still, to watch, and to listen." Ralph's lips were stretched in an uncomfortable smile. "So shut your mouths."

Two large brown girls hawed from the back row. Sit still with those drums chewing up the blood? Weren't the drums banned from the plantations? Banned from the ships? The slave owners in the big house couldn't stand their subterranean thuds. Drums banned. Pulse banned. Blood banned. Dance banned. That's why the hand jive was invented, because the slaves could quickly make their fingers quit dancing, hide them if someone heard the noise.

Whap.

Aisha started dancing the way she always did. Walking quickly in a circle. And the other dancers followed, echoing her movements just seconds after she gave the sign. Aisha sang out African words for them to repeat, *chena, tema,* words that meant "white" and "black." Soon the girls in the audience picked it up too, so that all the voices in the room were repeating the phrases. Even Ralph.

Chena! Tema!

Chena! Tema!

Then the room began to move, thirty women sitting, eight dancers dancing, three drummers drumming. Everything began to vibrate. The graffiti moved up and down and so did the bars, bending, melting in place.

Whap. Wha, wha, wha, whap.

As the pressure built up from underneath the floor, first through the feet, through the torso, and then out the top of the head, Ralph gave an assenting nod that the prisoners could join in with the dancers. Chairs were pushed back, and the circle widened to fill the room entirely with bodies jumping.

"Hey, sister, you really white?"

Sonny beamed.

"She sure don't move white, do she?"

A tradition of the circle dance is that anyone in the circle can jump into the middle. After Sonny and her partner had danced into the circle for their duet and returned to a place on the outside, two tough black girls sprang into the center. They were both tiny, with stringy bodies and faces like masks, and they generated movements that went from snake to antelope to cat. The movements interpreted the steps of evolution across the entire Serengeti. They crouched, their bodies touching, and the curve in their backs ascended from tortoise to lion. They stood up, their bodies still touching, and their arms extended laterally in the flight of flamingos. The walls fell away. The roof disappeared. The bars melted. The bricks dissolved. Whatever was happening, no man-made law could touch it.

"Stoooooppppppp!" Ralph shouted in his toughest voice. He had to yell it again to make himself heard above the din.

Whap. Wha, wha, wha, whap.

Everyone came back to the room, the hour, the place. The landing was abrupt and unpleasant.

Whap. Wha, wha, wha, whap.

Ralph mopped his head with his handkerchief. His shirt showed spots of perspiration. His eyes were confused, and his lips were curled back again in an uncomfortable smile. "You girls want to thank all these fine dancers and drummers for coming out here from Oakland today. Give them a hand."

The applause was thunderous and didn't stop until Ralph gave another threatening shout. "We're sorry to have to cut it short, but we've already run over our time."

The inmates filed back through the metal door, waving and shouting all the way out.

"Bye, sisters."

"Come back, sisters."

"You beautiful, sisters."

"Thank you, sisters."

"Love you, sisters."

"Sister, you sure don't dance white."

The metal door closed behind them but their voices were still audible.

"Love you, sisters."

Ralph escorted Aisha, Sonny, Eddie, and the others back into the van, out to the guardhouse where their exit entailed another inspection to make sure no stowaway was hidden in a conga.

Silently they drove down the highway past San Francisco, across the Bay Bridge to Oakland.

Yacuba's face pressed against the neighbor's screen door. He waved his woven African rattle at Sonny, "Mama. Mama. Mama."

Sonny picked him up and hugged him as tight as he could stand. If his daddy made it out of jail alive, maybe they could even have a life.

"Maybe," Sonny whispered.

Yacuba's mouth sucked on the top of his mother's cheek like a popsicle.

"Honey, they said I danced like I was black," Sonny's voice raised up into his ear. Her tears mixed with his saliva. She couldn't have felt more happy with him in her arms. "Like I was black."

The Duncan Dancer

YVETTE SETTLED BACK on the chaise lounge. She closed her eyelids for a short doze. The light behind the darkness shifted to a winter day in Paris as she and Randolph walked along the Seine and turned up Rue Jacob towards the Cluny. Everything in the picture was underlit, from just around each edge.

She and Randolph were walking and talking about the light. He had been asking her if it didn't make people less graceful to live where the light peered at you gloomily.

"We're dancers, and these things affect us. The dankness settles in my bones. It makes me ache in my sleep. I long for the light of the Aegean, the warmth of Greece." When Randolph talked to Yvette, he kept his eyes and mouth turned to the side, away from her. "But I am learning to appreciate the subtleties of such skies, aren't you?"

The conversation dissolved into a whisper, and they disappeared into the Cluny.

Yvette fell then into a deeper kind of sleep where

the images of dreams have no language to describe them.

The dance the next day was to be a celebration of what would have been Isadora's ninetieth birthday. Yvette's older sister, Yvonne, had arranged the party. Seven young dancers would be there to demonstrate Isadora's original choreography. Skip, turn, leap, and frolic deeply. They would wear the traditional Duncan tunic — loose, regal, feminine. Most of the dances would be combinations of circles, the girls holding hands and going around like the decorative borders of an amphora.

After the young dancers were finished, Yvette and Yvonne would perform a solo in honor of their beloved teacher. There would be flowers to litter the lawn and cake for the spectators.

For decades Yvette had tried to educate the public about Isadora's dancing, but the world persisted in only caring for the sensationalized events of her life — her illegitimate children, her Bolshevik affiliations, her affairs with poets and millionaires, her freakish death. These were common knowledge. But of Isadora's dancing, her dream to bring liberation and a natural grace to dance, people remembered nothing.

"Like the freedom of a bird in flight," Yvette heard Isadora's words of encouragement and stirred in between the satinet pillows. No one else, except the guards, was in the Cluny. The halls and rooms were empty. She and Randolph walked quickly to the tapestries, the soles of their boots clicking on the stone floor. Yvette stood before the woven figures of the virgin, the animals from the woods, the birds from the heavens, the unicorn bowed in reverence. She shed her coat and boots like an artificial skin, and in her pale blue diaphanous drapery, barefoot, Yvette began to dance. Randolph stared at the cloth on the walls, then at the young, earnest girl.

"You're going to get pneumonia and ruin your year."

"For the freedom of a bird in flight," she whispered.

He smiled to the side, averting his eyes, and summoned her to stop.

Yvette put her coat and boots back on. The picture of the unicorn faded, and instead she saw the weavers' hands shuttling the colors across the tapestry cloth. Then, slowly, the picture began to unfold itself. From line to line, the conception embodied its own realization.

"We can come to the Cluny everyday and see the evidence of this great effort, but all the moments that Isadora danced, they are lost to us forever."

Isadora's ninetieth birthday party would take place in Golden Gate Park in the Garden of Shakespeare's Flowers. This small protected lawn was bordered with the flowers mentioned in Shakespeare's writings. Lilies, lavender, roses, rue.

Yvette planned to wear her print chiffon gown, carry a blue silk scarf, and arrive barefoot. She turned her puffy body over on its side. After the dancing, there would be champagne toasts and they would troop over to the restaurant on Clement Street and eat Russian piroshkis in honor of the absence of their dear Isadora. Yvette heaved a sigh into the cushions of the chaise.

In Paris that year the Coq d'Or had been a favorite place for Isadora's dancers to gather. Borscht was fresh daily and the Rumanian violinists made their strings as sad as the cry of an abandoned child. Isadora was always eager to talk about Russia and the great Revolution.

"Not even at home, not even in America, can they understand what I am doing, but in Russia they know what it means to feel." Isadora took Yvette's hand and squeezed it. "They feel so much themselves."

Randolph stood, "A toast. To Lenin, to Lenin."

"To the people," Isadora joined in. "To dance and to revolution. To the freedom of a bird in flight."

They stayed at the Coq d'Or into the early hours of the morning. If Isadora had money, she stayed until it had all been spent, until she and the company were exhausted.

Daily the students gathered in the great rehearsal hall. Opposite the row of French windows was a magnified drawing of a Greek frieze, the hands of the three Muses linked. Next to it hung a poster of a Russian peasant. Isadora cried, she coaxed, she implored.

"Dance with your hearts." She said the words as if they were a song. "Dance with the light and fire of the Russian people as they marched through the bitter winter light, marching for a right to bread, up to the iced palaces of St. Petersburg." She cried again, "Dance with fight in your hearts—for freedom!"

Yvette leaned against the red flock walls of the Coq. The wicks of the candles were almost consumed, the bottles of vodka and champagne empty. Nearby, the waiters sobbed along with the violins and took the drinks that Isadora offered. Momentarily, they were consoled by the attention of the young American dancers dressed in Greek tunics.

"And isn't it a pity, enough to make us weep, to know we shall never set foot in our Mother Russia again?" The waiters dashed a glass against the wall for their memories.

Yvette woke up with a belch. She pulled a dressing gown over the rolls of her body and shuffled out to the kitchen. Past the yellowed photographs on the walls and the yellowed paper flowers in the vase by the phone. She took out the bread for toast, put on the water for tea.

"Like the freedom of a bird in flight."

Through the squares of lace on the apartment window, the curious downtown skyline of San Francisco shone like a toy city of steel. As Yvette padded her way from one end of the tiny kitchen to the other, glimpses of her reflection mixed with the flecks of neon, the spirals of office buildings, the lights from ships on the bay.

In the reflection Yvette caught sight of her face turned up to the gray Paris sky. She was tucking her scarf around her neck as she and Randolph walked from the Cluny towards the Luxembourg Gardens. They glided up Boulevard St. Michel as if they were on ice. Yvette looked at Randolph's delicate hands, reddened from the cold air. She was nineteen, and as she stared at the veins visible in his wrists, she made a note that she would never forget this day. The picture of his hands shivering in the late afternoon light would stay in her mind always. She would love his hands, love him always.

"You've forgotten your gloves at the museum. Shall I run and get them?"

Randolph shoved his hands into the pockets of his overcoat. "Tomorrow. When we go back tomorrow."

Yvette and Yvonne had been exceptional young women, leaving home without permission to follow the notorious Isadora Duncan to Europe. The Isadora who danced practically naked and fraternized with revolutionaries.

Yvette sighed over her warm tea. If only Randolph had laid his chiseled hands in her lap, placed his forehead on her shoulder, let her hold him. Yvette had amused herself for fifty years with the notion of taming Randolph, of releasing in him an unknown strength. But then, what did she know? She had been so young, so impressionable, and he had thought of her only as a child, one of Isadora's creatures. What use was it going over and over that day at the Cluny as if it had meant something more to him?

Yvette rolled her red hair up in curlers and wrapped a nylon net around her head. The curlers squeezed the sides of her face like the hat on a potato-head doll. The smell of burned toast filled the kitch-enette, and on the bay a tanker passed through the Golden Gate. She smeared cold cream across her cheeks and eyelids to remove the faded traces of makeup. The creases in her face were deep, and she had to pull the skin apart to wipe off the excess grease. She reached into the medicine cabinet for the blue bottle of rose water and dashed a few drops on her neck before going to bed. It made her feel less lonely to smell an odor different from her own. As she crawled onto the soft mattress and pulled the covers over her, the city winked through the crack in the heavy curtains.

Randolph was standing behind Yvette at the Coq d'Or, describing the Cluny tapestries to Isadora. No matter how hard Yvette tried, she couldn't make the voices go away. "One realizes," he droned, "that Christ was the last animal sacrifice of the antique world. The Mediterranean altars, red for so many centuries with lamb and bull and goat, were satiated once and for all by the ultimate sacrifice of the cross. Once the animal in us was tamed, the course of physical feeling was stoppered by the Church. It is for all of us," and here he had looked directly at Yvette for the first time, "to reinvoke the purity of feeling that comes from naked animal grace." Finally Randolph's voice drifted down into the street and disappeared with the roar of a motorcycle.

Yvette's stomach turned over in butterflies for the next day's birthday celebration. Flickers of her and Yvonne skipping through the Tuileries, throwing each other imaginary balls and feathers over the pools, around the fountains, tossing imaginary crumbs to the bewildered pigeons. Life had been so springy. Days dancing, nights dancing, museums with Randolph, coffees, wines, crepes, chestnuts, the aromas of the different restaurants.

"It's safest to learn geography in the kitchen," Isadora was fond of saying.

Each meal reminded her of a story, about the peas-

ants of Greece, the emperors of China, spies, dia-
mond cutters, princesses, thieves. Stories she had
lived or heard or invented. Stories of the days she
nearly died or nearly loved.

In the morning Yvette looked out the window at
the fog rolling out of the city towards the hills of the
East Bay. It was going to be a perfect day. She felt it in
her bones. "Bones good for something yet," she
laughed out loud.

At the dressing mirror Yvette applied her foundation and rouge, topped by a douse of porcelain white
powder. Over her buried blue eyes, she drew lavender shadow. She carefully made an outline of her
lips with a soft pink pencil, then filled in the rest with
lipstick. Her hair was its usual mess, but that was her
intention – to appear as a sea-born Aphrodite, a god-
dess who had just spent the last millennium riding on
a shell across the Aegean.

Yvette smiled at the picture of her face. "It's a
remnant," she thought, "but I'm there all the same."
And as she said these words, a pride filled her and she
looked beautiful to herself. She looked as she felt, the
bearer of Isadora Duncan's legacy. One of the last
originals.

Yvette chucked her breasts into a brassiere. She
pinned the bodice of her strapless gown to her underwear and wrapped a floral scarf around the strap to
hide it. Then she secured the contraption with a pin
of dime-store rubies. This was her only piece of jewelry. No bracelets, no rings, no interruption to the flow
of the arm. The gift of that flow was to remain intact
as it initiated from the shoulder blade and poured

down the arms and out the bouquet of floating finger-tips.

"The upper back should feel like one still had angel wings. The hands should caress the air like branches of seaweed." These were Isadora's instructions.

Yvette raised and lowered her arms. Flesh hung like soft, buttery fins from their underparts. Yes, the old feeling was still there. Her entire arm reached out in an offering. She felt Isadora's radiance fill her up. "I will dance today with inspiration. I will, I will."

Yvette put her wallet, key, and comb into a beaded opera purse, and into a paper bag, she put a sweater and socks for the afternoon chill that would roll back in with the fog. She fetched her slippers and walked out of the apartment into the fresh morning air of the city. Today, San Francisco even smelled like Paris.

The florist had saved Yvette a bagful of rose petals and two corsages of tiny sweethearts, pink for her sister, yellow for herself. Holding the bundles of flowers like a bride, Yvette walked slowly down the steep hill on California Street to the taxi stand.

"The Garden of Shakespeare's Flowers, Golden Gate Park." When Yvette spoke, she affected a slight accent.

The cab swung around to Fell Street, riding the rollercoasting hills west towards the park, the ocean, and the end of the city. San Francisco had been Isadora's home, or actually Oakland across the bay, where the fog was heading right now, dissolving over the suburban orchard that had been the Duncan place.

Before Yvette had come to San Francisco, she could remember the descriptions Randolph and Isadora had drawn of the drastic hills, the ferry rides across the bay, the ballet school, the dedication of Mrs. Duncan, who rode with her daughter across continents because she too had believed in Isadora's dream.

"Like the freedom of a bird in flight." That had been the dream.

Yvette rested her head against the back of the taxi. Perhaps she would ask the driver to circle around by the conservatory. To wait a moment while she went into the great white glass edifice to see the orchids and begonias. After all, it was a birthday for her and Yvonne too, for all of them who had loved and believed with Isadora. And for the young girls now who believed again.

Randolph and Yvette sat close together in the back of a Parisian cab as it raced along the Quai d'Orsay. They were on their way to meet Isadora, and it was drizzling and cold. Six communists had been arrested in the south of France, and Isadora was planning to raise money for their defense with a recital in protest of their detention.

Randolph was complaining, "I'll never be right again until we get back to Greece."

Yvette watched him stretch his fingers back towards his wrist. She let her glove fall on his arm as he continued to talk. "Once the whole spirit is engaged in an act of art, the soul frees itself from physical bondage in the body." Suddenly Randolph's face turned from the window of the cab and faced Yvette. "We must extend our dance towards this expression." His head twisted aside out towards the river, "Mustn't we?"

The cab wove among the traffic around the wide boulevards of the park.

"It's through those trees there, lady, the Garden of Shakespeare's Flowers." The driver flipped the arm of the meter up to its resting position. "Three dollars even, lady."

A great sigh came from the back of the cab. Yvette's head lay against the seat, and dozens of rose petals lay scattered on the taxi floor.

"That'll be three dollars even," the driver said again.

Yvette's ears were deaf, her eyes closed, her body inert. Yvette was dreaming again of the only life she had ever lived.

The Snow Dancer

A BOY NAMED Gateau LeFranc lived on a large island in the Caribbean Sea. The island was covered with volcanic rock and mountains, rain forests and dry stretches of plains, and clusters of towns along the shore where Gateau and his mother had their house.

Except for few, everyone on the island was poor. They survived by growing garden vegetables and catching fish, bartering for canned goods and salt, and earning tips at the large hotels near the water. They worked as waiters and chambermaids, cooks and laundresses, cabana boys and bartenders.

The tourist business was not so good the year Gateau turned sixteen. People from the United States didn't want to come to the island. The tourists didn't want to look at the little ragged children who hounded their evening walks. And the boulevards that connected the hotels to the sea were crowded with the residents from nearby tenements.

There were many other islands like Gateau's, covered with large trees and flowering vines, where the sandy beaches were even wider, where there were new hotels and fewer people. This year the tourists had decided to go somewhere else.

Now Gateau's mother worried that she would not have enough sheets to iron. Gateau worried about the price of fish.

Gateau thought that to worry so much was not a good life. He asked his mother what she knew about America.

"America is New York. It's a tall city, bigger than this whole island, and everybody rich there. Even colored people rich there."

"And everybody want to go there, no?"

"Yes, course they do. They want to drive big cars. They want to eat chicken every night. Course they want to go there."

"I want to go there too."

Gateau's mother smiled at her son with a face full of pity. "Every boy on this island say that to his mother. Sure as I sit here and look at you, they say it. But how you think you go? You think they go? They stay here like good boys."

Gateau went to his hammock. The moon hung low in the night like a silver spoon. Gateau dreamed of it pouring over the United States of America. It poured out from a big pitcher of milk and New York glistened all white in the middle of the sea. In his dream Gateau tilted up his face to the moon and moved his feet from side to side. In the dream he felt as if everything were white and he was waltzing. There was music in the dream, the kind of piano sound that came from the bar at the Tropicana. It was cold and white, but he was warm as he moved around in a circle.

When Gateau woke up, he was happy. He worked for his mother all day smiling, no matter what she told him to do.

Gateau's mother watched her son daydreaming. She let him be – working and dreaming. She didn't say a word. Instead, she sent him twice to town, and he didn't complain. She told him to shovel out the pig stall and whitewash the wall by the garden. She lent him to their neighbor, Michel, to clean his fish. Gateau, he kept smiling with his dream locked inside his head.

"Gateau, you been smiling all day. That's true, isn't it?"

"Yes, Mother."

"And you been dreaming too, haven't you?"

"Yes, Mother."

"Then, tell me, what you got inside your head?"

Gateau left the table. He backed up to his hammock and slipped across it like a scarf. "I got a woman on my mind. Don't pay it mind, Mother. It'll pass like the day in the night. It'll sink with the moon in the sea."

"Who, child? What you telling me?"

"Nobody I know, Mother. Just someone I see on TV. An American, as brown, as young as me."

Gateau's mother went out to the well. She spoke to the other mothers. "My son, Gateau, all he think about now is going to America. And your Jacques and your Pierre, they too?"

All the mothers' heads swayed from side to side with the pity and the humor of it. "They all gets it like malaria. They all wants to go to the United States of America."

When Gateau's mother returned to their house, her son was asleep. His smile glistened in the moonlight like an oar pulling through a phosphorous sea. Gateau's mother stood over her boy and looked at him.

She hadn't named him Gateau. His given name was Simon, like his father, but when he was a baby, she loved to suck on his fingers and hands. She always had some part of him near her mouth, kissing on him and chewing him, and to tease her, everyone called her boy Gateau, which means "cake" in French, the language of their island.

Even now she put one of his fingers softly in her mouth and said, "Good-night, Lord bless," and several other phrases meant to ward off any devil or disease that might come near him in the night.

For six months Gateau never stopped smiling. He smiled so much he looked like he was sick. And the more he smiled, the more his mother worried about him. She worried it was the work of the devil. That maybe her boy had sold himself for a ticket to the island of New York.

Through the rainy season, Gateau found work at the hotels. He worked hard to make his money during the day, and at night he dreamed of New York. One day he told his mother that he had secured a job on a fishing trawler.

"Now where you be going and when you be coming back?"

"Only for a week, Mother. For them to try me out."

"Who them?"

"Men from Saint Dominique. Black men and white men."

Before dawn the next morning, Gateau's mother walked with her son down through the town. The sea was as flat and black and still as an old mirror. Outlines of men hurried around the decks of the large fishing boats.

"That one," and Gateau pointed to the worn letters SOLEIL across the rusty bow at the end of the dock.

A young fisherman waved at Gateau.

"He be my baby," Gateau's mother said to the fisherman.

"Yes, Mother, we know. We takes good care of Gateau."

On board Gateau worked hard from sunrise until the equatorial fireball dropped into the sea. On the deck in the warm dark night he ate his dinner. Then he slipped into the cabin below, where the men played cards and repeated jokes. There Gateau laughed with the men. He drank rum. He listened to their stories about the whores of the Caribbean. He listened to their talk about the devils who ran the government on his island and the other islands. He heard them laugh about all the money in the United States, about all the women in Brazil. They gave him rum and promised he could come again with them to work.

The next week when Gateau returned to his own island, he was a man. Everyone noticed. His mother took him into her arms and then pushed him back with her hands on his shoulders. She looked at him and missed him at the same time.

"You not glad to see me?" Gateau teased his mother with his eyes.

"But you already gone again." Gateau's mother was less worried now. Gateau didn't smile all the time like an idiot. And she had made sure with the priest about the devil.

Gateau gave his mother half the money he made from his fishing trip, and the rest he buried in an iron box behind their hut. The next week he left again on the *Soleil*, and through the following months until hurricane season, Gateau went with the fishermen. Now he played cards with them. He visited the whores of the Caribbean. And he complained about the devils who owned his island.

"I go to the United States when I get the chance. I go to New York."

"There lots of money there, Gateau. Lots of money, but not so good as you think."

"My mother say that too."

"You good boy, Gateau. You needs to listen to your mother."

It wasn't money that Gateau wanted. It was the possibility of—he didn't know what. Possibilities that went beyond his imagination. He was in love with a place the way others are in love with movie stars.

On Gateau's island, the tourists had come back. They had grown bored with the smaller islands. Although pretty, there weren't so many people on them, and the tourists were lonely. They missed the parades of little children, the small bands of musicians in the streets, and the lively noises from the tenements nearby.

When the fishing boat was hauled up for repair, Gateau worked as a taxi driver around the island. He drove the tourists from the airport to their hotels and then around the town, out to the farthest beaches, and up into the mountains that pointed to the sky like rockets.

"Your island is very beautiful." In many languages the tourists told him. He liked the words in English. "Beautiful," he repeated, and they were charmed by his accent and the whiteness of his teeth. Gateau made good tips and decided to give up the fishing trade.

"New York is an island too?" He said to the Americans in his taxi.

"But not like this. Nothing like this."

Gateau closed his eyes to the stars. He tried again to imagine what kind of island New York could be.

Buildings a hundred times taller than the largest hotel and so close together that no vines, no trees grew between them. Throngs of people, crowding into trains under the streets. Big stores and markets, hundreds of movie theaters. And weather that took months to change from hot to cold to hot again.

In his mind Gateau saw the city and it was shiny. All the buildings were hot and brilliant in the sun. Then the sky became gray. Leaves were swept off the trees and white powder came out of the sky. The air was cold but the snow made a blanket over the whole city. Gateau could feel himself covered with soft, wet cotton while everything around him on the island was white and silver under the moon.

Gateau was a man who had one dream, and he walked it like a tightrope. Looking neither left nor right, he walked with the knowledge that one look would pull him down to the ground. Into the ground of this island that had already swallowed his father, his grandfathers and grandmothers, their fathers' fathers and mothers. And buried with each went the hope of returning to the continent of Africa and home.

Now Gateau wanted to take the culmination of their dreams with him to another place. He listened carefully to his heart. It only beat with this mission. He knew it. His mother knew it too. Afterwards, he could marry. Later, he could have children. Until then, Gateau kept to himself. The friends of his mother asked her why such a good and handsome boy not want to marry their daughters.

Gateau's mother shook her head. Inside she was proud.

Gateau knew how much it cost to go to New York. He knew how much it took to get a visa. Little by little, he saved enough.

"You need a coat, Gateau."

"What?"

"I make you a coat so that when you go to New York, you stay warm."

"It cold there now, Mother?"

"Gateau, there be no way we even know how cold it is on that island."

Gateau looked at his mother gratefully. He be going and she still be taking care of him.

The coat was made of layers of cloth, some cotton,

some wool, some silk, laid across each other and quilted together. The outside was red and the inside was black. It was loose across Gateau's shoulders.

"When you get to the island of New York, you buy a sweater and put it between you and that coat." Gateau's mother held up her hand. "Then it fit you like this."

II

Gateau planned to get work, to stay, to make enough money to send for his mother, to live in the United States forever.

"But here on the island they don't let a young man go. They want him for the fields or for the army. They ask, 'Where you get the money to fly to New York?' They say you must have stealed it. Then they take it. They put you in jail for thieving. It not so easy to go to the United States."

This is what the fishermen told Gateau. "It's not enough to save your sou. You have to have a reason for going."

Now Gateau didn't smile. And that night he didn't sleep. He walked outside his house, down to town, back to the pier, out to the end of the beach, where new hotels were under construction.

In the morning his mother took his hand. She held it up to her lips, "You lose your dream? Where your dream?"

Gateau's words spit out of his mouth, "In the fist of the visa man."

"Yes, yes."

"He maybe don't let me go. He maybe take my money."

"Yes, yes."

"He maybe call me thief. He maybe send me to jail."

Gateau's mother rocked him with her voice. "You'll think of reason to go. Reason the man can't refuse."

Gateau placed a wool blanket in the bottom of his bag. He laid his extra pants, his shirts, his handkerchiefs and socks on top. In the back of the house his mother made a big breakfast for him—fried plantain, fried fish, fried potatoes. Gateau carefully tucked the sheet of paper with his cousin's name and put it in his shirt. Even if he lost the paper, he knew the street address by heart—Maurice LeFranc, 349 West 147th Street, New York City in the United States of America.

The hat on the visa man was tipped back from his forehead, and drops of sweat hung onto his eyebrows. He eyed Gateau indifferently. He was impatient for noon. Gateau hesitated for one second, and then approached the man. One hand was in his pocket, holding his money, and the other held onto his red coat.

"I want to go to New York today," Gateau said softly.

The visa man surveyed Gateau's red coat. "No one goes on the day he asks to go," he said looking through Gateau's body at the clock on the dingy office wall.

"I need to go today."

"You need?" And there was mockery in the man's voice.

Gateau's body hung silently inside its clothing. Not even his heart made a sound.

"Why you want to go?"

Gateau held out the money for his visa and extra for the visa man.

"Why you want to go?" The visa man sounded angry. He pushed Gateau's hand and the money away.

Gateau cupped his money against his chest and said, "I need to see my cousin Maurice."

The visa man stood waiting.

"Maurice drives a taxi in the city of New York. He already been there ten years."

The visa man looked at him disdainfully. "Go home, Monsieur Gateau. There are no visas for America today."

Gateau trudged back through the town, carrying his coat and suitcase, past the large pink hotels, up to his mother's house.

"No good?" She shook her head.

"No good."

"Tomorrow you try again. Tomorrow you have reason to go to New York."

Gateau didn't unpack. He didn't eat. He hardly spoke. In his own mind, he had already left. He wasn't even there.

At nine the next morning, Gateau walked towards town again. This time the visa man looked Gateau up and down as if he were a foolish person and then smiled. "Bonjour."

Gateau didn't reply.

"Bonjour," the visa man dared Gateau not to answer.

"Bonjour," Gateau placed his bag along the side of the wall. He walked towards the visa man with the money in his hand. This time the wad for the visa man was fatter than the day before.

"So tell me, why you want to go to New York today? Your cousin sick?"

Gateau glared at the floor and then lifted his raisin eyes face-to-face with the visa man. He picked up his coat, he grabbed his bag, he walked out of the small cement block building into the main square of the town. The reflection from the whitewashed facades blinded him. Gateau looked at the sea. He looked at the sky. He looked at the flowers, the pink and purple and coral bougainvillea that splashed along the walls of the town. Then he went home. He went to the hammock outside his hut and cried.

Gateau's mother came and stood over her son. She lifted one of his square brown hands to her mouth. "Poor baby, poor baby. In your mind you already flown away, but your stubborn body still here."

Gateau's mother sat beside her son. She hummed a lullaby and watched him fall asleep. She too believed that Gateau was going to take everyone from their family with him to America. And that nobody's ghost would rest until he got on that plane.

Late in the night Gateau raised himself up. He washed his face. He washed his entire body. He ate his dinner like a horse. Then he went back to his hammock and slept past noon. When he got up again, he ate like two horses. He told his mother that he was going to take his body to America.

When Gateau entered the shabby emigration office, the visa man was slouched in a swivel chair playing solitaire. He looked up and smiled at Gateau like a friend. Gateau walked towards him. There was no money in his hand today, and he had left his bag and coat outside the door. As Gateau got closer, he could see the grease spots on the visa man's uniform and smell the tobacco on his breath.

"You still want to go to New York?" The visa man's voice was small and hollow.

Gateau nodded.

"Then tell me a good one. Tell me why you want to go today."

Gateau's look asked a question of the visa man's face, asked if there was hope that they could for a moment share something. Then Gateau's eyes closed and he said, "I want to see snow."

There was a moment of silence. Gateau held his breath. Then the visa man's mouth opened like a fissure. "Me too." Something cold melted in the visa's man face. "I want to see snow too."

He reached out towards Gateau's hand and counted out the fee for the visa. "Today, huh? You want to see snow today? Yes, yes, it cold there now. It maybe snowing this very day."

Gateau's head wagged idiotically. It was still moving when the visa man disappeared into the adjoining office. During the eternal thirty minutes it took for the visa man to return from the back, Gateau lost his senses. He was crazy with joy and terror, alternating and at the same time.

That night Gateau boarded his first airplane and

flew into the dark sky, over his island and the other islands hovering in the sea like giant turtles.

Through the night he watched, his head pressed into the glass of the window, for the island of New York. At dawn the pilot announced they were going to land. Gateau could see nothing of the city, the buildings and streets, the crowds of people, the maze of taxis, the harbor of ships. There was nothing but a bank of clouds. The pilot guided the plane through the thick, white covering to the other side, where the skyline of the island of New York leaned against the sky. Gateau cried with the beauty, and as he left the plane, his head lifted up to the sky, his feet shifted from side to side, and on his face for the first time he felt the wetness of falling snow.

The Converted Dancer

THE ENGLISH CHURCH of the late Middle Ages had three things it feared most for its nuns. These were known as the dreaded Ds – Dress, Dogs, and Dance. There were no other aspects of secular existence that could so undermine the purity of female life in the convent as the three Ds. No doubt because the Devil was a D himself.

At the nunneries the Ds were well known and highly discussed. "These are desires that will surely tempt you into frivolity," it was explained. "And although avoiding fancy dresses, little pets, and dancing alone cannot guarantee you heaven, following the Church's rules against such frippery is an excellent start towards your salvation."

It was all because of the ladies who came to the convents on a temporary basis. These ladies came for many reasons. Out of shame or out of sorts with their fathers and husbands. Needing refuge and shelter, these women regarded the sanctified walls as hotels and brought their stylish wimples with them. For company they brought their dogs, who took the pillow next to theirs, since the Crusades for Sangreal had carried off their suitors.

Even before Polo and before the prominence of Venice and Lisbon, England was getting ready. Hundreds of years in advance, the Crusades were preparing Great Britain to be an empire. And the ladies were preparing themselves for the long-awaited return of their lords or, at least, a confirmation of their death.

So it was that dozens of them, with their fortunes and their fondness for the Ds, found their way into the chilly gray cloisters of the Middle Ages. These women usually stayed at the convent where a younger sister was a noviate. With too many girls in a family and only so many suitors or so much dowry, the youngest often found herself a nun, with no inclination or longing for that deposition.

*

It may sound irreverent but such a girl was my sister Anne, only fifteen and already signed over to God. She had been sent from home only six months ago when she received news that I, the middle sister, Gwendolyn, was to arrive for a visit to the priory.

When Anne first caught sight of me, my profusion of hair, my lovely velvet robes, my terrier Armand, I felt Anne's own timid disposition take courage. She stuck her hands into the folds of Armand's belly. She stroked the fur on his back and the thick material of my skirt.

"I regret for the third time this week that I ever was

born to a life that offers a promise of warmth only in the Kingdom beyond."

The prioress had commanded me to be cautious in displays of affection or conversation with my younger sister. "Since Anne has already shown such a steady and thoughtful bearing, it is important to remember how delicate an age fifteen can be." It was requested that I keep a distance from Anne's preparations for holy life.

"My dear little Anne, my dear little potface." I stood an inch above her and brushed her bleached and unlined cheeks. "Dear little potface," I murmured her childhood nickname.

We buried our heads in each other's shoulders and remained silent for several minutes.

"For joy," Anne pointed to the tears that splashed across her chest.

Later, Anne was reprimanded, and the prioress requested another word with me.

"There is no reason to jeopardize your sister's salvation. Do not incline her to a longing that cannot be hers. Your life and your own salvation are in the hands of God. He will be merciful. Let Anne rest with deep content that the life Christ our Saviour has chosen for her is the most blessed. Do not tempt her with stories that arouse covetousness. I pray for your soul, for Anne, for us all. But here I am protected by the roof that is our cross. I would not want the decisions of a world of sin."

For me there were long walks in the countryside with Armand. I gathered bouquets of dried leaves, spent hours on the embroidery frame, and hours at prayer as well. Meals were silent, simple, plain, and dull. I barely had more than a chance to nod to Anne.

After I had been at the priory several weeks, my sister and I had an unusual moment alone. She was breathless with urgency. "Listen. I pray you, listen. You and Susan I do dearly love. And Mother, whom I wish could press me again. Dear Papa, whom I shall join when Mercy has closed my life." Anne heaved out the phrases like stones pitched from a quarry, "Our cats and horses, the food and feasts, I miss with all my heart. But I have come to understand, even in this short time, that the world is something I shall learn to live without.

"However, in the night I still tremble," Anne looked around to make sure no one watched us, "with fear that I can never abandon the impression of our birthday parties. All the dancing we used to make. The fancy French cakes. The gifts. The singing bird Uncle brought us from the Holy Land, a place they say lies next to a sea as blue as a robin's egg, as flat as a glass.

"The dancing moves me most of all, even in my dreams. I fly out the window of my cell to the pastures beyond the moor, and there I move with my feet to a tune that comes out of the stars."

A smile that lifted only the left portion of Anne's mouth spun across her face, then instantly fell away. She said gloomily, "I have transgressed and will have to confess that I did utter D. Twice I uttered D."

After this outburst, Anne found occasions to talk to me about life at home. Four years apart in age and tempered the same, we looked at each other across an opening that tunneled back between us to a rich and mannered life. Memories we shared from our former existence with each other – our young friends and tutors; our animals and walks; our giddiness at festivals, at marriages; our journeys to Oxford, Canterbury, and London; our adoration of Missie, our nurse. We recalled playing by the trench that ran around our manor house, riding out to hunt, preparing for visitors, learning harp and needlework. The memories of long days rolled across our minds, endless and the same, passing through into the present.

"And the serfs," she said, "their lives, like mine now, always looked no different going forwards or backwards."

Wicked as it may sound, I decided to make a plan. I was determined to take Anne home for the occasion of her sixteenth birthday. Under the pretext that our eldest sister Susan was ill, I said that I was obliged to go to her side.

"And if Susan were to die," I convinced the prioress, "Anne should be there too, as the sibling chosen for life on earth closest to God in heaven."

So it was arranged. Anne and I would travel a day, a night, and a day to our home and to the side of our sister. We would both return as soon as we were able.

"You are not to forget how much the convent needs your good thoughts, your generous heart, and your busy hands." The prioress lightly kissed Anne's forehead as we took our leave.

When we arrived home, much had been prepared, much was in preparation. Anne was shocked at my lie, relieved to see Susan well, and overjoyed to be home. She behaved as if a spell had been broken and went sprightly through the hallways humming.

"She's humming," I said to Susan. "That alone assures me that the lie was justified."

Anne busied herself with the inspection of the land around, stopping by springs and ponds, by willows she had danced under as a child. Quite unused to spare moments, she took advantage of them to sit quietly, looking out through the casement windows to the fields. At night she dreamed of her body moving, her arms lifting under the trees, her bare feet springing on the grass.

For Anne's birthday, Susan and I draped the upstairs gallery with colored scarves. We bustled about, insuring that "potface's" favorite dishes were prepared in just her favorite way. We arranged bouquets of flowers and a woven wreath of primrose and lavender for Anne's cuff.

Our little sister was as excited as a nightingale, hopping from one corner to another, kissing nieces, allowing herself to chatter.

What conspirators we were, offering Anne trinkets of affection and a puppy to take back as a donation to the priory.

Anne hushed any thought that here with her family, with us who had loved and raised her up, she might be committing a transgression in the real eye of her Lord.

"The three Ds be ignored, O Jesus, for just today."

After courses of soup and meat, oranges, nuts, and cakes, toasts to Anne's health and all our long lives, a group of musicians, dancers, and jugglers were ushered in.

At birthday parties in the past, Anne was always the first to join the jangle of tambourines, flutes, bells, and drums. Now it was entirely against the rules of her training to publicly admit a desire to dance.

Anne imagined that the sight of her in the cloth dancing would make everyone cover their eyes and run. Or incite the Devil himself into a duet. Her dancing would cause the signs of Jesus and his Church that covered the walls of our good house to crumble into ashes. Her dancing would cause us all to fall into hell.

Anne said, "A sin against God to be his dancer."

The performers formed two lines, inviting the seated party to join them. Susan and I declined. Everyone declined. In respect to Anne, none of us danced.

We tried to persuade Anne to stay a few more days. "What does it matter?" I asked.

"And when is it in this time of Crusades and war that we can all be together?" Susan begged.

Anne agreed, "Surely a few more days is harmless enough in the eyes of the Lord."

Anne reassured herself that she hadn't danced. No, since the day of the beautiful party, she hadn't even hummed. "I have breathed, and let that be miracle enough that I survived the spectacle without bringing ruin on my family's head. Although the temptation flooded me, I repeated silently the account of Christ in the desert, when the dancing Devils came to eat at his Holiness, too."

Susan took dreadfully ill the day Anne and I had planned to return to the priory. She had fever and chills, lesions and boils, and there was no way to keep food in her.

We put off our leave again, sending word to the mother superior that Susan's condition still required our attention.

It did indeed. Both of us stayed constantly by Susan's side at prayer. Three days later, our dearest sister was dead.

As soon as Susan was buried, Anne said she was desperate to return to the company of the nuns. It was at her departure that I was struck with the thought that Anne had found her calling.

The Belly Dancer

Two dilapidated Volkswagen buses bumped their way over the ruts in the road until it ended. There at the dusty terminus of the nine-mile track stood a couple of wooden sheds, a crumbling adobe house, a dry well, a pile of old tires, and the remnants of a barbed-wire fence.

Behind the abandoned settlement were the ruffled slopes of the mesa. To the west of their jagged outline, the sky exploded with gigantic bolts of red and purple fans. To the east the world had already gone under. The air on one side held a hush, anticipating the moisture that the plunging temperature would bring; while the other side of the horizon was still wagging its hot and noisy fingers, dense sherbet cones that would finally melt into the mauve underground. The last light would be neon green—a celestial phenomenon evident in New Mexico—and the hot brilliant day would suddenly disappear into a cool brilliant night.

Like the island tropics, where the sky decides to gulp and the sun falls down its throat through a hole in the sea, high desert sunsets leave only a moment to appreciate their racing splendors. In an instant the scene is barely a shade lighter than the gray night-hawks splicing the air.

The group of women jumped out of the vans, sucking in the fresh air and attempting to make saliva in their dry mouths. The heat and dust on the ride out had required that the windows in the vans remain shut. As airtight as possible. Even so, a fine film of dirt had settled on everything—their hair and skin, their teeth and tongues, their eyelids, clothing, and food.

Becca shaded her eyes against the glare of the setting sun, lifted the water bottle out of the van, and passed it around to the other women.

"Her tribe," she called them.

Their first task was to unload the vans. Sleeping bags and blankets, food and drinks, suitcases filled with costumes, baskets of musical instruments. The second task was to haul in dead wood from the groves of piñon and scrub oak that grew nearby. Becca assigned each woman a chore and tramped off with a hatchet over her shoulder into the brush to find kindling.

The women hauled the sleeping equipment down the hill behind the abandoned house into a small basin of land that lay up against the mesa. The cooking area would remain above by the vans, but for protection against the wind, they planned both to dance and to sleep in this hollow

The moon was on its way up, fat and taxi yellow.

The full moon of September. It rose up over the tentacles of the Sandia Mountains and poised as big as a giant ball in the sky. The big rocks that surrounded Becca's descent into the copse of trees went from magenta to mud as big *luna* pressed her cheek against something deeper than blue. Arabian blue and horses and nights swept across the American desert, and Becca could be heard shrieking the infamous cry of the tribeswomen of North Africa.

"Lalalalalalalalal." High-pitched and unearthly.

Her tongue flapped against the roof of her mouth like a broken shutter, "Laalalallalallallalalalllallala." The sound contained the name of Allah himself.

At the bottom of the hill ran an arroyo. Famous everywhere in the Southwest, these arroyos are dusty circuits of rivers hardly ever seen. Only when heavy rains certify these ruts and turn them into water dervishes do they run high. Then everything in their way – trees, sheep, cows, cars, houses for those ignorant enough to build in an arroyo – is swept away with them. They are dangerous, even murderous when ignited, but usually they are inert, a part of the arid terrain.

Tonight bone dry. For twenty years this particular riverbed, wide enough for a boat, hadn't run a single drop. On one of its useless banks grew several huge cottonwoods. These woody green trees had sunk their roots deep into the underground waters and grown large enough to embrace the moon. The September moon had risen and gotten smaller, as polished and dainty as an old dime. Below it, the rocks looked high silver and the leaves on the cottonwoods shimmered.

The dance outing had been Becca's idea. She had drawn a picture of the full skirts of women twirling. "Like the Seven Sisters, the Pleiades in the sky. Our tribe." Above the dancers was an outline of the mesa and the moon. "Our dance for the full moon of September."

Becca was the group's teacher. She was the eldest, anticipating her fortieth birthday at the end of the month, hoping for a child by the summer solstice. She had been blessed by St. Christopher and consequently traveled everywhere–trekked in Nepal, lived on the Costa Brava, walked across Sumatra, journeyed to New Mexico to visit D. H. Lawrence's ashes in Taos and stayed.

"That's it. I'm home."

Becca stayed to learn about the Indians and the proud descendants of Spaniards who settled to the north. Stayed to gather the herbs and flowers that only thrived in the desert. Stayed to learn the art of healing with teas from old Hector Martinez in Santa Fe. She had affixed herself to the landscape with no intention of going anywhere else ever again. Now she wanted a baby to share her settled life with. Not a husband, but a child.

Just as Becca had found her way to New Mexico, the others had found their way to her. They were her students at the Middle Eastern dance class she taught out in Albuquerque's North Valley.

When Becca found herself in the great American desert, she ritualized her days and nights around the celebrations of the belly. "The abdomen where nourishment is taken, the womb where life is conceived," she said to her students. Movements simultaneously innocent and sensual. Movements that came directly out of the deserts of the Middle East.

The belly dance originated in the desert harem to mitigate the pains of labor. It marked the contractions for the Praise-be-to-Allah child newborn to the desert tribe. Belly dancing was originally an exclusive female activity and took place in the privacy of the female quarters.

As the stomachs of the women rolled in unison with the laboring wife, their motions could be said to mirror the landscape outside the tents. A landscape that showed a camel train moving slowly, undulating over the dunes, over the mounds of sand. A picture of roundness within roundness. The sky was a bowl, and the desert was a bowl.

Eyes from the tents followed the series of camel humps across the horizon to the date palm oasis. The eyes saw that everything was softened by the curves of the animals in the bowl of the land. The men that walked beside their camels moved slowly. Time moved slowly. The horizon went on and on. The roundness of the earth went on and on.

Below the mesa, the winds were blowing the landscape from one place to another. The women covered their eyes with their hands. The dirt whirled mercilessly, whipping their skin as they piled back onto the pillows in the back of one of the vans.

The wind spun the ground so hard that the mountains, the mesa, the sky which was still day on one side and night on the other, disappeared. The air became a solid bank of rust.

Becca's ears strained against the window of the bus. The sand scratched at the paint and glass. Everyone's mouth had started to turn dusty again. Shivers of fear ran in a circle from woman to woman. The bus rocked like a cradle and the air thickened.

Becca closed her eyes and saw the opaque black cloud of a genie emerging from a bottle in a shroud of smoke, threatening to kill the poor fisherman who had set him free. For centuries the genie had lived at the bottom of the sea, hoping to give his liberator any treasure he desired, but so much time and so much waiting had elapsed that the genie had changed his vow of generosity to one of revenge. The poor fisherman hovered with fright.

Becca and the other women were also locked in a tin vessel on a landscape which resembled the bottom of a large sea. The water was long gone, but the remnants of the ocean were trapped in the fossilized rocks of the desert. The howling and rocking continued, and each of the women tried to reckon with the unleashed forces outside the membrane of metal and glass. One sat very still, listening to her own heartbeat. Another shifted around restlessly, wanting to get out and run in the storm. One thought the winds were punishment for her sin. Another worried about her daughter at home. One was plain scared. But Becca was assured that the powers of their dance, their womanhood had brought on this elemental recognition and approval.

For an hour the brown cloud surrounded them. Nothing was said and each of them sat with her head buried in her palms, eyes closed, waiting. Then the sound of the storm stopped. The wind vanished, the air instantly cleared, and the moon and stars popped out in the sky.

Becca opened the doors of the van, and the women jumped out, stretching their cramped limbs, grabbing woolen sweaters, socks, gloves. The wind had disappeared and left behind a temperature nearly freezing.

Over thermal underwear they began to dress. They pulled on long satin skirts and slipped on dazzling metallic corsets made of coins and chains of gold. They covered themselves with embroidered velvet vests. They fastened veils across the lower parts of their faces and wound scarves around their arms and waist. They unfastened wide money belts and hooked them just below the hips. They removed jewelry from their bags, elaborate silver filigree necklaces and assorted bracelets. They took off their hiking boots and put bangles around their legs, toe rings on their feet.

Their fire blazed under the night. Once the flames burned down, the cast-iron pots of chile were placed on the coals of piñon wood. They brought out the wine, opened the bottles, and passed them around. The sound of finger cymbals and drums turned everyone's attention to the center of the circle.

> *O Mother*
> *you whose body*
> *we give service to*
> *in our dance*
>
> *We pray that you help us*
> *generate a light*
> *as powerful*

as beautiful
as your own

And that through our dance
we return to you
our shining gratitude
for your presence

   The waves of bodies began to pour through the air. Regulated by their breath and the music from their feet and hands, the bellies swelled like storms at sea, then spun in towards the center, a vortex of sinking skin. Tidepools of flanks, branches of arms rippled in attendance to the full anemone in line above them.
   Lalalallalallallallallallalla.
   Their prayer was for each other. For the moon. For the wild light in the sky and the shadows that swerved in and out of the circle. For hair and skin and its variations. For the color of henna and the mark of kohl on the eyes. For things familiar and strange, invented and natural, the young women, the white American tribe, jangled their brains senseless.
   There was barely a pause in the movement. And above the sound of their breathing, nothing could be heard except the drums and the skipping of bare feet. The air that moved the cottonwood trees was no longer separate from them or from anything around them. Animal, vegetable, mineral. Their sight was blurred by a unified vision of matter passing into light, their bodies passing into an uncommon state, an unusual suspension, more fluid than solid. More consuming and more consummate. The women had

drowned in the depleted oceanic cauldron of the desert floor. Called grace by religions, witchcraft by economies, initiation by societies. And blasphemy, insanity, loose.

While the women danced, the moon dropped behind a mesa peak. The night darkened, and the approaching howl of the coyote was swamped by the dance. The four-legged fugitive circled the rim of the small valley, walking swiftly around the rocky edge. His voice had dissolved into a low and continuous tone.

Lalalalalalalalalalallalala.

The sounds from the coyote's throat could have been the voice of a hundred, a thousand beasts. It only served to amplify the thousand sounds around him and, consequently, was inaudible.

Suddenly and at once like the storm, everything stopped—the women, the drums, the coyote. The dancers stood frozen and their sweaty eyes looked up to see two pieces of gold shining down at them—animal eyes. The mouth below the ducats opened in a grin, and a set of pointed teeth glistened—animal teeth.

The creature ran skirting the rocks at the top of the hill, coming towards them, drawing away. He laughed, he snarled. Except for the heaviness of the women breathing and the voice of the coyote, there was no sound.

Shadows entered shadows and the coyote's eyes shone like searchlights down the hill.

Lalalalalalallalalalallalalalalla.

Becca stared at the spot in the sky where the moon

had been. It was their dancing that had invited the coyote to the rim of the hill. It was their powers that would keep him from harming them.

The coyote made one curious lunge forward, and the women took one step back. He headed down the rocky slope and paused by their vans. The fire crackled, and the coyote bowed his head politely towards the women. Becca bowed her head in return and began to move towards him. As soon as he sensed her approach, he ran off, disappearing into the tunnel of the night.

The moon had traversed the sky. Becca tapped the tambourine, making a faint jingle in the morning light. It was barely dawn, and the others were sleeping. Their bodies looked as if they had thrown themselves down in place. Bright scarves crisscrossed the dry ground like silk bridges.

Becca shivered. She stood up and stretched her arms towards the tops of the small cliffs. She stirred the coals under the chile. The air smelled dank and sweaty. Tiny bird peeps came up from the ground and down from the puffed-up cottonwoods.

Becca fingered the satin folds of her skirt, holding for a moment the deep sense of completion from their dance. Despite the inhospitable wind, despite their strange visitor in the night, they had danced for hours – softly and wildly.

Now she was certain what it meant. These things were signs – like everything else. Signs for fullness and abundance, signs of life's surprises, signs that next September when she returned to dance with the moon, it would be a celebration for the birth of her child.

The Modern Dancer

Dear Ted,

I wish I were feeling better. I'd put on a mazurka and dance on top of the furniture. Oh, that's a good idea I've had, isn't it? A stage full of old, sagging armchairs, the upholstery torn, the springs hanging out the bottoms like droopy drawers, and dancers leaping from one to the other. All men, Ted, in homage to you.

The electric company called today to terrorize me. I told the woman—she said her name was Mrs. Moped—I was helpless and to take it up with my caseworker. For God's sake, what do they expect me to do? What would you do, Ted? Legally, they can't do anything but threaten, so why am I even pretending to be scared. (I guess I'm scared of everything these days.)

You missed the invention of the VCR, Ted. It's one of the greatest advancements of the century—especially for the sick, the wounded, the infirm, the dying, the aged, the lame, and the weak. Dig this – I'm too tired most of the time to get out of bed so I look up movie titles in the brochure of my local video rental store. Ted, you can't imagine. It's better than delivery pizza, take-out Chinese. I can rent any movie I feel like seeing. Last week I visited the Wild West and, of course, I was thinking about Loring's *Billy the Kid.*

On the VCR you can stop the film at any point, rewind, and watch again. In *High Noon* I rewound one scene several hundred times to study Gary Cooper's walk. I thought, put that walk in a 2/4 tempo to a slow electronic version of "Home on the Range," six from stage left, six from stage right, Lee jeans, bare-chested, walking in a swagger towards each other, one leg extended in a synchronized slow turn, arms relaxed. I can see it clearly, Ted. It's a beautiful dance.

I told Mrs. Moped that if they want to harass me, they'll hear from my caseworker. She'll call Mrs. Moped and give her hell. However, I'd be terribly inconvenienced if they shut me down. In the meantime I could freeze to death. I can imagine the obit in the *Voice* – "Promising Choreographer Dies of Exposure." Ugh!

Anyway, the video store makes home deliveries to a little locked box outside my door. They even bring popcorn.

My friend Sarah was in a car accident in February and is now paralyzed from the waist down. I only heard about it last week, right before I left to go to the clinic. It was me her father called in 1971 to deliver the news that her brother had been killed on a motorbike in West Virginia.

Last night I dreamed about S. I had gone to visit
her, and she was living in a bright apartment in the
suburbs. She had a baby grand piano that she had
learned to play. I called her this morning to tell her
about the dream, and all she said was that she wanted
to kill herself.

Oh, God! My neighbor's third-grader discovered
something dreadful last night. The Top 40.

Speaking of dreams, Ted, I dreamed that you were
biting the back of my neck, standing behind me,
loving me powerfully. We were looking at a map of
the world. You were dazzling, dressed like a samurai.
You pointed to an island southeast of Japan and said,
"We should go and live there."

I was in the country when I dreamed this. It will
probably be the last time I'm there, but I don't want
to think about things that way. Believe me, I still have
hope. Maybe heaven is in the country. Don't you
think that it is both the most elevated and the most
idiotic characteristic of man to have hope in a hope-
less condition?

My friend James refuses to get the test. He doesn't
want to know. He says his ignorance is his bliss. I've
never not wanted to know anything, even the most
painful, the most humiliating, the most frightening
sorts of things.

Anyway, I was visiting in the Berkshires, not far
from the Pillow, and I slept in a little trailer under
enormous black oaks. Sheep in the meadow, cows in
the corn. I tramped with friends across untilled green
fields with swaths of bright yellow buttercups, violet
lupine. In one afternoon we had hail, cold and bitter

winds, hot sun, rain, rolling clouds, the whole season of spring in a couple of hours. And beyond the meadows in the distance was the peak of Mount Washington.

I wished I had known you, Ted. I often feel I do.

This may sound shocking, but I don't much believe in evolution. You know, science's insistence that one kind of animal led to another. I just don't see it. First of all, when a man is compared to an animal, it's usually an insult to the beast. Take that neighbor child, for instance, the one who tunes in to the Top 40. She's a little wolverine, but really there is no mammal except human who could tolerate the noise she listens to. Thump, thump, thump.

When it comes to the significant differences between us and other primates, I can accept that our vertebrae straightened, that our brain enlarged, that we even moved from signifying to poeticizing language. But the thing that baffles me most—and it's a chasm of difference that strikes me as unbridgeable, (I don't care who the lost link was)—is sex. Yes, Ted, how is it that humans found such elaborate and profound pleasure in an essentially biological activity?

Yes, yes, I know there are complicated mating rituals in the animal world, but not in the act itself. Once the mating decision is made, the act itself is perfunctory. Everyone laughs when I get started on "My Exquisite Exposition." Although it's killing me, I'll go to my grave believing it is a divine activity to share the pleasures of the human body.

It's what I think dance is all about too.

When I get tired of watching movies, I lie around

making up dances. I wrote one or two down I want
to tell you about. I spend some part of every day
blocking and reblocking, changing details in the costumes and set, casting different dancers. I call this
new one *Who's Who in Shoes*. The entire backdrop of
the stage is a wall of shoe boxes. I love that image,
don't you? Shoe boxes from floor to ceiling.

When I was a child, I remember the mystery of
those rectangular boxes—each marked with size, col-
or, and style, the coded combination of numbers and
letters that barely hinted at the inside. Ted, my mother had such shoes—backless and beaded, gillies with
grosgrain bows, fur slippers, velvet evening shoes,
brown and white spectators, pony skin pumps, al-
ligator t-straps.

Anyway, on stage in front of the stacks of boxes is
a couple waltzing barefoot. The music is atonal.
Weird music, Ted. I'm not crazy about melody. (Re-
minds me too much of Illinois.) The dancers begin to
examine the shoe boxes and try the shoes on. They
even dance "wearing boxes without topses." I love
this intro and in my mind it could go on and on—
around the world in shoes. They exit and the music
shifts to cello, harp, viola.

There's a story here, Ted, and I'll get to it in a
minute. I'm so tired that I think I'm going to have to
nap before I finish this.

This disease is a terrible thing. No one should have
to die of pleasure.

Two hours later. Much better. Even the view of the
building next door offers a possibility.

I know you weren't crazy about modern modern dance, but some of it is really fabulous.

Last winter I saw a group of young dancers downtown. Can't recall their name now or where they were performing. The female dancers were in harnesses suspended from the ceiling. They could fly, yes fly–up, down, across. They were dressed like angels–wings, diaphanous, everything. I swear I cried, Ted. They hovered over the males stretched out on the floor as if they were dead. Oh, it was passionate, as good as Limón.

I hate the way the word *meaningful* is thrown around. You know today "meaningful" can apply to a PB & J sandwich. But the work has to be committed to saying more than just something about itself. I know you'd agree.

After the intro, a single dancer appears stage left on point–fuchsia toe shoes. I call her Ruthie. She's carrying hat and dress boxes. She's a customer in what we can now presume is a shoe store. She is devastating–haughty, spoiled, privileged, mean. Face it, Ruthie is a real bitch. She is interested exclusively in two things–herself and shoes.

Whenever I write something, I have to give the dance parts names. Not #1, #2, #3 dancer but names. That's why it's easy to write to you because your name means so much to me.

Lily, the salesgirl, appears stage right–barefoot and dressed in a long flannel smock. Her musical theme is wind–piccolo and flute. I always found it so charming the way Prokofiev attached an instrument to identify each character in *Peter and the Wolf*.

Lil begins to attend Ruthie, undoing her satin fuchsia toe shoes. She holds Ruthie's shoes like precious objects. She dances with them in her hands and drifts to the back of the stage.

Lily pulls out box after box, brings down pair after pair of shoes for Ruthie to try. But there is nothing suitable, and Ruthie is furious. Is it starting to focus for you?

Ted! Ted! Ted!

The people around here try my patience. The avant-garde is terribly clever at calling attention to themselves but, finally, so what? So what if someone can stand on her head, playing the bassoon, surrounded by a chorus of female tap dancers while a video camera documents the event as Art. An abbreviation for Arthur, right? Anyway, I hope *Who's Who* tells somebody something.

Did I mention it? My mother is coming next month to take care of me. I'm not so bad off yet. I told her, "Wait," but she's insisting. She's been living in Phoenix for almost ten years and she's flying out here. She says Grandma's coming too later in the year. I'm a little worried about the mix—Mother, Grandma, and my leather boyfriends, but Mother has a good attitude.

Of course, she's going to faint when she sees how thin I've gotten. Her cooking should improve my appetite, although everyone has been doing a champion job nourishing me—dropping off chocolate truffles and banana milkshakes in the middle of the day, taking me out for spaghetti and meatballs.

My friend James escorted me uptown last week—

he had a two-for-one coupon for spare ribs, corn on the cob, hush puppies, turnip greens, and sweet potato pie. Apparently, soul is having a revival on the West Side. He talked about whether he should get the test or not. (As far as I'm concerned, it's not a topic for debate.)

One thing I forgot to mention is the shoe bench with a slide attached to its front. Every time Ruthie tries on a pair of shoes, she lifts her foot onto the slide while little Lily fits her. Then she takes off in different steps, different poses. There's an exaggerated classical theme as the bitch gets bitchier and Lil gets frantic. She's searching boxes desperately now, finding objects of all kinds – vegetables, kitchen utensils, parts of dolls, hardware, maybe a cat, things unsuitable to the shape of rectangles. A struggle over one of these objects ensues, and Lil drives a spike heel into Ruthie's heart. In this case, you'd have to say the customer is not always right, but dead. Ha, ha! That's the ending as it stands. What do you think?

One of the problems I struggle with is the old chicken-and-egg dilemma – too much form dries out the eye, too much content detracts from the purity of expression.

There's a second ending I'm trying on. I know it sounds like content overload, but listen. Halfway through, a man enters. His name is Ernst, and he's a bit of a sleaze. We've seen him earlier in the prologue, dancing with Lil, going around the world in shoes. Ernst is the manager of the shoe store, a Taurus with Leo rising, and he wants this Ruthie to buy, buy, buy. He wants to please. While he dances with Ruthie, waltzing her this way and that, Lil, *la miserable,* takes a spike shoe and impales Ruthie on it. (The shoe I have in mind has a three-inch lucite heel, and the nails which connect the heel to the sole are visible through the plastic. Every time I think about that shoe as a weapon, I start to laugh.)

Lil drags Ernst off the body, and there's a lot of gymnastic back and forth here. It works up to an apache à trois, and Ruthie really gets jiggled around. It sounds a tad silly, doesn't it?

Let's see. I've told you about my mother, the problems with the utility company (thank God, the landlord's a decent guy). I mentioned food and movies and *Who's Who in Shoes.* My health I touched on briefly and lodged two complaints against the neighbor child. There's not too much else people talk about these days.

The end isn't far. I can't count it in days, but I'll be lucky to live more than a couple of years. A few months down the road, I may think I'll be lucky to die. Yes, I have a lot of problems right now. You can imagine how terrible it is to be an invalid—not to turn, to lift, to jump, not to be dancing. But the mind is as strong as ever. Maybe more so.

Ted, I have to tell you. I've just started to work on a second piece. I put the first mark on the blueprint yesterday—it's the sound of vacuum cleaners and the gestures of housework. A few years ago I did research on the movements of work. You know, the hunters and gatherers didn't swing their hips in dancing because their daily tasks didn't require much lateral motion. But in agricultural societies, it was necessary to bend the upper body across the lower half to plant and harvest crops. These work patterns then became incorporated in sophisticated dances, most prominently in Africa and Indonesia. I'd like to do a series of American dances based on work, using industrial sounds, etc. Vacuuming is just the beginning. Exciting, huh?

I'm so glad you're there, Ted. Or rather, here. I don't think I could ever exhaust the things I want to tell you. I have a photo of you by the bed. It's a constant inspiration to me—one of determination and grace. It's hard to stay determined when you're sick. That's why it's true that if you have your health, you really do have everything. I have less than that now. My spirit is determined, but my body is a rag.

Well, enough complaining. I'll go sleep off this fatigue and get back with you later. There's leftover lasagna and half a bottle of wine. My toast will be to you, Ted, and the endurance of your work.

Dear Ted, I wish I wasn't going to die.

About the Author
Summer Brenner has performed, taught, and extensively
studied flamenco and contemporary dance. She is the author
of two books of poetry and a novella, *The Soft Room* (The
Figures Press, 1981). Her work has been included in *Deep
Down: The New Sensual Writing by Women* published by Faber
& Faber and *Up Late* edited by Andrei Codrescu. She current-
ly lives in Berkeley, California.

About the Book
Dancers & the Dance was designed and formatted by Allan
Kornblum at Coffee House Press, using the Ventura Publish-
er book design program on an Epson Equity III+ computer.
The compugraphic version of Eric Gill's graceful Perpetua
type was provided by Stanton Publication Services in Min-
neapolis, Minnesota. The book was printed on acid-free
paper and smyth sewn into wrappers for added durability.
Printing and binding by McNaughton & Gunn in Ann Arbor,
Michigan.